Indoctrinaire

Also by Christopher Priest from Gollancz:

Indoctrinaire
Fugue for a Darkening Island
Inverted World
The Space Machine
A Dream of Wessex
The Affirmation
The Glamour
The Quiet Woman
The Prestige
The Extremes
The Separation
The Dream Archipelago
The Islanders
The Adjacent

Indoctrinaire

•

Christopher Priest

This edition first published in Great Britain in 2014
by Gollancz
An imprint of the Orion Publishing Group
Orion House, 5 Upper St Martin's Lane, London WC2H 9EA
An Hachette UK Company

1 3 5 7 9 10 8 6 4 2

A CIP catalogue record for this book
is available from the British Library

ISBN 978 0 575 12119 5

Typeset by Deltatype Ltd, Birkenhead, Merseyside

Printed in Great Britain by CPI Group (UK) Ltd,
Croydon CR0 4YY

www.christopher-priest.co.uk
www.orionbooks.co.uk
www.gollancz.co.uk

PART ONE

The Jail

One

•

The gale howled across the frozen plateau. Born in a cyclonic whirling of clouds in the southern Pacific Ocean, fifteen hundred miles from the Chilean coast and a thousand miles to the south of Easter Island, it spun off polewards in a wave-flattening thrust of freezing air. Gathering momentum it roared across the floe-specked Amundsen Sea, and plunged through the obliquely angled terminator into Antarctic night, the winter night when nothing living should ever move across the surface of the land. The wind battered itself against the face of the coastal range of mountains, tearing off sharp-edged fragments of ice and hurling them on southwards towards the plateau and beyond.

In the lap of the plateau, a mean five thousand feet higher than the frozen surface of the sea, the wind took on a relentless quality – a storm-wind moving in an unfaltering blast across the ice-slick surface, touching velocities of a hundred miles an hour, or more. Human flesh exposed to it would crystallize, break and crumble, then disintegrate in minutes. No man could stand the cold for more than seconds.

This was the first gale of the winter.

Six hundred feet below the surface, on the rocks of the plateau itself – rocks which had not felt the warm touch of the sun in millions of years, if ever at all – man had dared to build. Well lit, well ventilated and centrally heated, the Advanced Technique Concentration carried on its functions in perfect security and with absolute impregnability.

From the surface, the only signs of its existence were several well-stayed poles marking each of the access-shafts on the perimeter. In summer months there was an airstrip here, and sometimes in winter too. There was one more flight expected this year, when the gale had blown itself out, then no more for another five months.

The men in the Concentration needed the peace and security of the plateau to carry out their work. Here, more than four hundred scientists and their assistants worked on their specialist subjects – biochemistry, particle physics, nucleonics, bacteriology – usually in almost total ignorance of each other's work.

For the Concentration was no tiny station claiming a few square yards of Antarctic rock, but a complex system of research units linked by many tunnels through the ice. Its total area was thirty square miles, and it had been ten years in construction.

In one of the laboratories at the southern end, Dr Elias Wentik sat comfortably in a soft plastic chair, and fondled the muzzle of the rat which lay in his lap. The creature pushed its snout affectionately against his hand as he absent-mindedly stroked it.

His assistant, a tall Nigerian named Abu N'Goko, worked with his head bent over a desk untidily scattered with notes.

'We shouldn't stop now, Dr Wentik,' he said suddenly, looking up.' We can't afford to be restricted by a mere technical detail.'

'But there is nothing we can do about it,' Wentik replied mildly. 'No one here wants to finish more than I do.'

'You know that's not only what I mean.'

'That we're not going fast enough? We should find an alternative process?'

'Yes.'

I know you do, and I agree, thought Wentik. It is frustrating to be delayed for so long by something that is probably irrelevant.

Probably ... *Was.* Wentik knew that the blind alley they were in was only temporary, but the problem was whether to go on, or ... Or what? The alternatives frightened him.

He glanced down at the rat on his lap. In three days, or less, it would be dead. The drug worked on the creatures, and worked as it should. Yet within six days of the administration of the drug, all the treated animals died. Whether it was as a direct effect of the compound, or some side-effect caused by the metabolism of the rodents, Wentik didn't know. There wasn't another kind of animal in the Concentration with which they could experiment, and no more could be flown in until the end of the winter.

There was only one available kind of animal left to try it on – man.

For days, Wentik and N'Goko had argued it backwards and forwards. N'Goko wanted to go on; Wentik counselled restraint. Whereas N'Goko was willing to submit to experimentation himself with the drug, Wentik wanted to develop different varieties of it, gaseous and liquid, and wait out the winter until they could obtain different breeds of animal.

And anyway Wentik had tried the drug himself against his own better judgment, though he had not admitted as much to N'Goko.

For the last three weeks he had been taking minute quantities of it, under carefully self-imposed restrictions. He was always alone in his room with the door locked. He made sure each time of no interruptions, and would lie back on his bunk and watch the hallucinations it produced. For, like lysergic acid, the drug seemed to have no harmful short-term effect. Aside from its hallucinogenic properties, and the vivid dreams it sometimes produced after taking it, Wentik had been unable to determine any deterioration of his mental or physical make-up. Larger or more concentrated dosages were another matter.

He said to N'Goko: 'I know what you're going to say, and the answer's still no. You're not going to take the drug.'

'Is that final?'

'Yes. For the moment we carry on trying different strengths and mixes on rats.'

'And go on killing them,' the Nigerian said, slightly bitterly.

'If we have to.'

The two men sat in silence for several seconds. Finally, Wentik said: 'I wish we'd known this would happen before winter.'

With an abruptness that startled them both, the door banged open. Wentik whirled round angrily in his seat.

'What the hell do you mean by coming in like that?' he demanded.' This is a private office!'

There were two men standing in the doorway, neither of whom Wentik had seen before at the Concentration. The taller of the two men, who stood slightly behind the other, looked at Wentik with what was evidently keen interest. But it was the other man who spoke.

'Doctor Wentik?' he said in a voice which held a distinct quiver of suppressed authority.

'Yes. Now get out before we throw you out. You know the rules of the Concentration.'

The two men looked at each other.

'I'm sorry if we've breached etiquette, Doctor Wentik,' the man said.' But I must ask you to step outside for a moment.'

Wentik looked at his assistant. 'Do you know these two?' he asked.

'No. But they might have come in on the last aircraft.'

'That's right,' the taller of the two men said. 'It'll take only a moment.'

'What do you want?'

The shorter man held the door wider open and indicated with his hand that Wentik should go out into the corridor.

Wentik stood up suddenly, and passed over the tame rat to N'Goko.

'Look after Browning for a moment,' he said, using the pet name he had given to it. 'There's only one way to deal with this.'

His assistant took the rat, who squealed loudly at the disturbance. Wentik followed the taller man into the corridor, while the other shut the door.

'Right, let's see your ID,' Wentik said. Everyone at the Concentration was exceptionally security-conscious and it was unlikely in the extreme that anyone could gain illegal entry to the station even if they were able to find it. However, it would do no harm to flex the muscles of the rules.

The first man silently unbuttoned a flap over a breast pocket in the drab grey uniform he wore. He took out a green-covered booklet, and passed it over. Wentik took it.

Everything was in order. Below a photograph of the man was a string of numbers and the name: *Clive V. Astourde.* Several other details were printed on the page, but Wentik skipped them. It was only a formality anyway.

'What about him?' he said.

The man called Astourde said: 'I can vouch for him. He isn't carrying a card.'

'Then he should be,' Wentik said. 'Do you realize that if I were to call the Military Police I could have him arrested?'

Astourde nodded, and the two men walked slowly away. Wentik's ordeal had begun.

That was the first of three occasions he talked to Astourde before leaving the Concentration.

The second was in the tiny bar in what was geographically and socially the centre of the Concentration.

He and N'Goko were sitting at a table with some of the technicians who worked under them. It was informal but the conversation, as always, centred around their work.

In some ways, Wentik and N'Goko were unusual at the Concentration for they were the only non-Americans. Wentik had flown over from Britain a few months earlier on an exchange basis for one of the big chemical corporations in the States. Within weeks his work had been classified and he and N'Goko had found themselves working for a branch of the Administration. His transfer to the Concentration had been only partly voluntary, as by now he was directly responsible to a defence subcommittee within the Pentagon. What had started out as a simple piece of biochemical research had escalated rapidly into something whose full implications were still not totally conceived.

So what had been merely a three-month separation from his wife was now going to be at least another five months.

Astourde walked into the room, unseen by Wentik, and bought a small beer from the bar. He raised it to his mouth, sipped it, and walked over to Wentik's table.

'Do you mind if I join you?' he said directly, interrupting Wentik in mid-phrase.

'I'm afraid I do.'

N'Goko said: 'You're disturbing an important conversation, Mr Astourde.'

'What I want is important too.'

Wentik sighed, and said: 'OK.'

He moved to another table and sat down. Astourde sat beside him.

'Do you mind if I ask what you are doing here, Doctor Wentik?'

'I do mind, and I don't see what it has to do with you. What right have you to be here?'

'I'm on government business. I think you knew that anyway.'

Wentik said: 'I doubt if you could be here at all if you weren't working for the state in some way or another.'

Astourde smiled, and Wentik noticed for the first time the man's tiny eyes, reflecting the light-bulbs that hung from the metal ceiling. He reached into his breast pocket and pulled out a short strip of translucent paper. Within the fold lay a section of 35-mm film.

He tossed it on the table in front of Wentik.

'Take a look at that,' he said.

Wentik raised it to the nearest light-source, and peered at it. It was a single frame from a colour film. On the edge of the film, outside the sprocket-holes, were the letters *KODA* –.

The frame itself was a picture of a stretch of what looked like short-cropped grass or corn-stubble. The sky was a pale blue, crossed with a sharp white streak of jet-trail. Because of the size of the frame it was difficult to make out details, but not far from the camera was a white aircraft standing on the grass. It was of a design like nothing Wentik had ever seen before.

Astourde passed him a magnifying glass.

'Look at it with this,' he offered.

Wentik took the glass, and examined the craft in closer detail.

With no scale to measure by it was impossible to estimate the size of the craft. It rested on the grass without undercarriage, but its nose was raised a little higher than the rest of the body. Its shape was pointed. The only sign there was of a cockpit was a sloping piece of glass set flush with the lines of the rest of the fuselage. Although it was on the side of the craft it seemed to be the only part from which it could be piloted. The plane had stubby delta wings, set high on its body.

'What is it?' Wentik said.

'We think it's a jet aircraft of advanced design.'

'You think . . . ?'

Astourde said: 'It took off shortly after that photograph was taken. It was a VTOL. No one got near it.'

Wentik put the piece of film on to the table, and finished his drink. 'So it's a UFO. Why tell me?'

'Because it's not that. We know it's a jet, and that it's piloted by human beings.'

'So whose is it?'

Astourde shrugged, and finished his own beer. 'No one in the Pentagon can identify it. That's why we want you.'

He got up and walked away.

The last time he saw Astourde before leaving the Concentration, Wentik was back at work in his laboratory again, the day after the encounter in the bar. With his characteristically brusque manner, Astourde walked in and went directly up to Wentik. 'I must see you,' he began.

'I'm busy. You'll have to wait.' Wentik turned back to his work.

Astourde took his elbow in a firm grip and propelled him to the door. Outside in the corridor the temperature was at least twenty degrees cooler, and Wentik shivered.

Astourde said: 'We're leaving tomorrow.'

'We . . . ?'

'You and I. And Musgrove.'

Wentik turned sharply, as he realized that the other man was in the corridor too, dressed in black trousers and a dark blue polo-neck sweater. He was carrying a rifle, and held it at an uncertain angle in the fingers of his right hand, as if not accustomed to the handling of weapons.

Wentik said: 'But I can't leave. I'm in the middle of my work.'

'That's all been cleared from Washington.'

'You mean I'm being recalled? No one has said anything.' Musgrove stepped forward. 'That's why we're here. It's connected with your research.'

'In what way?'

Astourde said: 'You'll see when we get there.'

Just then, N'Goko came to the door of the laboratory and stood looking at the three men. In his hands he held the tame rat. It was dead.

Wentik looked at N'Goko, then back at the other two.

'Where are we going?' he said.

Astourde's hand moved towards the breast pocket from where he had taken the photograph the night before.

'To Brazil,' he said.

Two

•

My dearest Jean,
Well, I warned you I wouldn't be able to write much longer. But there's a plane coming in tomorrow against all expectations, so everyone is writing letters tonight. But surprise! I will be on the plane myself.

It doesn't mean I'm coming home just yet, but at least it looks as if I shan't be wintering under the Antarctic ice-cap! I'm pleased in some respects ... we're somewhat stymied on the work at the moment. I'll tell you the details when I see you, but for the moment all that has happened is that our tests on the rats haven't worked out quite as planned. I'm leaving Abu in charge here for the moment, though it doesn't look as if I'll be able to get back here until after the winter's over. Abu has all my notes, although I fear that once I am out of the way he'll take matters into his own hands.

But my other news is much more mysterious! It seems I'm being recalled by the government. They've sent two of the strangest men down here to get me. I don't understand Americans, but I suppose I never will. One's a very swarthy man called Musgrove, with big shoulders and arms. He doesn't say much but just hangs around and looks menacing. I saw him with a rifle the other day, but I can't think what he means to use it on. The other man, though, without doing anything positive really gives me the creeps. He has a rather disconcerting habit of walking away in the middle of conversation, as if he is striving for some kind of effect. I feel the whole time he is waiting for a chance to pounce, *though God knows he's got no axe to grind as far as I am concerned. Anyway, I expect all the mystery will be cleared up by the time we get to Washington. Though that's something else that's a bit odd. When I asked this man (his name's Astourde, by the way) where we were going to, he said Brazil. I'm presuming that he meant Rio de Janeiro, since that was one of our last stopping-off places on the way down.*

You're not to get alarmed by this, Jean dear. I'm sure there's nothing in it. It's just their manner that's so disconcerting. When I get to Washington I'll telephone you straight away, and it could be that you'll even be hearing from me before you get this letter.

I'm off to get an early night as we're leaving in about ten hours' time. The plane is due here in the next few minutes. Apparently it would have come earlier but for a gale that's been blowing for the last few days. We never get to know about the weather down here.

Give my love to Timothy and Jane. I'll get them some presents before I come back. And you . . . look after yourself, and don't worry. be in touch. 'Bye for now.

All my love,
Li

Three

•

Wentik lay in his hotel bed, and listened to the early-morning sounds of the town of Porto Velho. Already the muggy heat was rising along the banks of the Madeira River half a mile away. In the square below, a heavy diesel engine was continually ticking over with a hesitant repetitive sound.

For the last fortnight he had been here, waiting while equipment was flown in from the coast.

Astourde had disappeared. The man, incongruous now in the heat of the city in his thick grey uniform, took Wentik by taxi to a hotel and, without excuse, left him there.

An hour later, Musgrove had turned up. He was Wentik's only contact in Porto Velho, rarely leaving his side. He seemed to know little, and spoke even less. Wherever Wentik went, Musgrove followed him, and he began to get his first uncomfortable feelings of being not totally free.

His major discomfort in Porto Velho was his lack of information. All he knew was that Astourde and Musgrove appeared to be working for the American government, had possession of a photograph of an unknown plane, and were ordering and buying several tons of equipment like tents and food. This rather abstract disquiet, and the necessary boredom of hanging purposelessly around a South American riverside town, added to the slight feelings of disorientation he was experiencing.

Apart from this, his days in Porto Velho passed comfortably enough. Musgrove was the worst kind of companion (never volunteering information, and rarely supplying any even when asked) but his room in the hotel was acceptable, and his personal freedom comparatively great. Only when he asked Musgrove when he would be returning to Washington did the man show any streak of threat.

'You won't be going there,' he said, not looking directly at Wentik. 'Not ever. Nor will Astourde.'

The day after he arrived, Wentik wrote a letter to Senator McDonald, who was chairman of the Research Appropriations Subcommittee that handled the affairs of the Concentration. He stated exactly what had happened to him, and asked for an explanation. He wrote everything he knew about Astourde and Musgrove (which wasn't much) and told the Senator that he was being prepared for a journey whose destination he did not know. He closed with an urgent request for an immediate reply.

He managed to post the letter in a public square without Musgrove noticing, and in achieving this felt immediately more secure.

Only later, when the days dragged on and no reply was forthcoming, did his apprehensions return.

He heard the diesel engine rev up suddenly in the square below, then snicker down into silence.

Abruptly, with his usual disregard for privacy, Musgrove blundered into the room. He crossed to the bed and stood staring coldly down through the mosquito-webbing at Wentik.

'We're leaving,' he said curtly. 'There's a suitcase here for your stuff. Pack as few things as you can, then come downstairs. We're waiting for you.'

Wentik dressed quickly and, looking out of the window, saw that Musgrove was talking with a group of about twelve men. They were dressed, like Musgrove, in neutral grey which bore no insignia, yet had the unmistakable appearance of a uniform. Whatever the purpose of the clothes, they were totally inappropriate for the climate.

As he watched, the men loaded a few crates into a high-sided diesel lorry.

Wentik came downstairs, and joined the others. The men, evidently seeing him for the first time, looked at him with frank curiosity. Musgrove said something incoherent to them, and they climbed into the back of the lorry with the equipment. He looked sourly at Wentik.

'Are you ready?' he said.

Wentik nodded, and he and Musgrove climbed into the front cab, where a driver was already sitting.

Wentik found himself in the middle of the cab between Musgrove and the driver, sitting on the housing of the internally mounted engine with his legs astride the gearbox. Musgrove lit a black-papered cigarette, and the evil-smelling smoke drifted into his face.

The driver rested his elbow on the frame of the open window as they rolled slowly through the dusty streets. It was still only eight o'clock in the morning.

At the bank of the river they halted, and Musgrove went into the office of the ferry-company. Within minutes, the engine of the antiquated hover-ferry had been started, and they were taken across the river towards the uninhabited southern bank. Here, the ramp up from the water led on to a deserted highway cut through the forest. As the lorry drove away, the ferry swung gracefully in a cloud of white spray back across the river towards the town.

The road led south from Porto Velho, in a black straight line across the plain.

Wentik said: 'Where does this road lead to?'

'Bolivia,' Musgrove replied shortly. 'We don't follow it far.'

They followed it, in fact, for thirty miles, then on Musgrove's instructions the driver turned off to the left on to a one-way metalled track. Immediately, the going became more hazardous.

Occasionally they passed through tiny villages, where half-naked children would run down to the side of the street and wave. Even now in the late 1980s, thought Wentik, there were still places on Earth where a mechanized lorry was a novelty.

The day grew hotter, and the air coming in from the windows at the side did nothing to ease the growing discomfort in the cab. Around noon they stopped for a light meal and a drink, then they were on their way again. Wentik grew more and more conscious of the fact that they were striking away from the relatively civilized plain around Porto Velho and into the foothills of the high plateau that formed part of the Mato Grosso.

Towards evening, Musgrove (who had spent the major part of the hot day in brooding silence) reached into his pocket and passed Wentik a scrap of paper that had been folded many times. It was dirty, and bore the marks of several fingerprints.

Wentik opened it and started to read.

Elias Wentik:
You are probably mystified as to the nature of your journey and its connection with the photograph I showed you. I can only tell you to be patient for the moment. A lot of our so-called knowledge about the Planalto District is largely speculative, and much of its nature is self-explanatory. The machine in that photograph comes from the Planalto District; I took it myself on an earlier visit. More than this, you will discover for yourself as you enter the District.

Do not be alarmed by Musgrove's behaviour. He can seem a little irrational at times, but he will do you no harm. Anyway, I have charged him with your safe transit, and will hold him responsible if you do not arrive safely.

Yr obedient servant,
C. Astourde

'You've read this?' Wentik asked, holding it up.

Musgrove laughed. 'Yes. Astourde had sealed it originally, thinking I wouldn't open it.'

Wentik looked again at the piece of paper. The uneasy formality of the last phrase stuck in his mind throughout the evening. There was something derisory in its context, as if Astourde recognized a growing submission by Wentik to circumstance.

Beside him Musgrove chuckled, adding to his forebodings.

'Where are we going?' Wentik suddenly said to Musgrove as they squatted in the light of the oil-lamps suspended from branches above their heads. The other men had driven off in the lorry to the nearby village of Sao Sebastiao after pitching the tents and eating another meal. Musgrove was leaning against the trunk of one of the trees, idly listening to music coming through a battered transistor radio at his side.

He said: 'To Planalto.'

'Is Astourde there?'

'He will be by now. He's flying in by helicopter.'

Wentik pulled the letter from his pocket, and looked at it again for about the tenth time that day.

'What is the Planalto District?' he asked. 'Is it some kind of government base?'

Musgrove smiled enigmatically.

'You could call it that,' he said. 'The only people you'll meet there will be working for the government.'

'And the aircraft?'

'Astourde took that photograph the first time he saw the District. You'll find out more about that later.'

Wentik sat in thought for a moment. Around him, the noises of the dark Brazilian jungle went through their terrifying range. High in the trees, animal voices wailed backwards and forwards, sounding uncannily human. There was nothing like this in Wentik's experience: a constant ululation of sourceless banshee screams. Musgrove had told him they were harmless. In the jungle were a great many arboreal animals; in particular spider-monkeys and sloths. In this part of the world, animals are never seen, they are only heard.

Wentik looked at the other man, his face half in shadow from the inefficient lamps in the trees. Musgrove's expression was blank, like that of a man unwilling to divulge more information than he had to.

'What is the Planalto District?' he asked him.

'It's a region of the Mato Grosso. In English it means "high plateau".'

'Then what is special about it?'

Musgrove said: 'You'll see. It's a part of the world where you can see in one direction but not in the other. A place you can walk into, but not out of.'

Wentik stood up, inadvertently knocking one of the lanterns as he did so. Shadows swung around them in the clearing. Holding on to one of the low branches he stood over Musgrove.

'I don't understand.'

Musgrove stared up at him blandly and began rolling one of his black-papered cigarettes.

'You'll see,' he repeated.' When we get there.'

Suddenly irritated, Wentik walked away to his tent. Musgrove had been uncooperative and uncommunicative all the time he had known him; now he was being deliberately cryptic.

They drove for three more days, climbing higher and higher, and encountering steadily deteriorating driving conditions.

Wentik's first night under canvas had been a nightmare experience. The jungle was alive with insects and animals, and the cries continued from dusk to dawn. His face was spotted and swollen with insect bites, and the legs of his trousers were fraying already from the sharp and densely matted undergrowth that was everywhere.

Musgrove took delight in pointing out the more horrific indigenous fauna. They passed a pool at one point, swarming with frogs five and seven inches long. Their passing disturbed the reptiles, who let out a croaking roar whose suddenness and volume had startled Wentik. A column of *sunba*-ants had crossed the trail, and Musgrove directed the driver to stop while they watched. When the stream of insects was at its widest, he nodded, and the lorry drove through, crushing the inch-long insects with a clearly audible crackling noise. Behind them, the column marched on unbroken.

On the second day the track ran parallel with the indistinct bank of a wide, yellow river. The rain-forest they had encountered in the foothills had now given way to dense tropical jungle, the sky rarely visible overhead. It rained for hours every day, a warm muddy rain that only increased the overall humidity of the jungle and did nothing to cool the temperatures. Everywhere was a dank, sweltering green. The trees themselves seemed to be made of mould, as if no timber grew inside their trunks. Everywhere, parasitic *liane* creepers sprawled across branches and trunks, as if to drag down the jungle to the humus-flooded floor from which it grew. In several places the creepers had grown or fallen across the track, and the men had to hack a way through with the razor-sharp *machetes.* Brightly coloured parakeets flew from tree to tree, a dazzling burst of movement that seemed out of place in these monochrome surroundings.

The men in the back of the lorry took it in turns to drive, but Musgrove and Wentik were always in the cab. The heat was intolerable. Wentik had no change of clothing and within a day of leaving Porto Velho his clothes were drenched with sweat.

The track had now become nothing more than a flattened, muddy path through the trees. The lorry lurched constantly in and out of slime-covered pot-holes, and the never-ceasing rocking in the cab was extremely uncomfortable to Wentik, perched precariously on the hot engine-cover.

Musgrove lapsed again into silence by the evening of the second day, as if sensitive to the irritation he had earlier caused Wentik. He'd swear occasionally at the lurching of the cab, but beyond this said little.

Only once since the first night was the subject of the Planalto District raised.

Wentik had said: 'When do we get there?' Mysteriously, Musgrove had thought slowly about his answer, then said with his sardonic crypticism: 'That's right.'

Making nothing of this Wentik had let it go, and said no more.

On the third day they came across the wreck of an American army-lorry, standing with its nearside wheels in a pool of stagnant water not far from the road.

The driver of their lorry drew up a safe distance from it, and the three men in the cab climbed down. There was no sign of anyone around.

They climbed into the compartment at the back and discovered a diesel compression-generator and several assorted excavating tools ranging from hydraulic machinery down to spades and picks. Musgrove looked at the lorry impassively, and scribbled into a notebook the number stencilled in white paint on the nearside running-board. They returned to their own lorry.

Before getting into the cab Musgrove climbed into the back, and Wentik heard the groan of a hand-generator of the type used on short-range radio transmitters.

Five minutes later Musgrove was back in the cab, and the lurching trek through the jungle continued as before.

That afternoon, after several miles of extreme difficulty, with the engine and gearbox roaring in low-gear four-wheel drive, Musgrove suddenly pointed across the cabin and shouted at the driver.

'There! Park there!'

The driver braked immediately, and the lorry jerked to a halt.

The men in the back climbed down, looking dirty and tired after what must have been a long ordeal in the box-like compartment at the rear of the vehicle. They unloaded several small crates from the lorry, and shared them out between themselves. Wentik was given two rifles to carry, and a canteen of luke-warm water. Musgrove helped himself to a huge duffel-bag containing blankets.

Laden down and sweating profusely, they all set off on foot through the jungle.

'Stop!'

Musgrove's voice brought them to a halt. Apparently unhindered by his unwieldy load, he'd stepped out several yards ahead of the others. Now he stood with his arms apart, silhouetted against brightness ahead.

He turned and called to Wentik. 'Come over here.'

Wentik gave the two rifles to the nearest man, and walked forward.

Musgrove turned as he reached him, and looked at the other men. He seemed undecided about what to do.

Finally he said: 'I think you'd better go back to the lorry. Work your way round the perimeter until tonight, then in the morning join us at the jail. The map-reference is in the folder.'

He tossed a compass to the man who had been the last driver of the lorry, then nodded to Wentik and they walked forward.

They moved for several hundred yards, the light ahead of them brightening slowly. Wentik, curious to see what the source of the light was, had difficulty in keeping up with Musgrove, who, in spite of the customary tangle of undergrowth, was moving positively and quickly.

Then they reached the edge of the forest, and stood looking across a broad plain. The sun shone down brilliantly on close-cropped stubble, hurting their eyes.

The photograph ...

That colour-frame Astourde had carried had been taken here. In the centre of one of the densest jungles in the world, a plain of mown stubble that stretched beyond the horizon.

Wentik looked to his side at the trees, and noted how abruptly the terminal line between trees and stubble was drawn.

'What the hell is this place?' he said to Musgrove.

The other looked at him derisively. 'What you've been waiting for. The Planalto District. Come on.'

Together they stepped out of the jungle, and walked across the plain two hundred years into the future.

Four

•

They had walked for about three hundred yards, when Wentik turned to look back at the jungle they had left. It had disappeared. Behind them, as in front, the stubble extended to the horizon.

Shaken, he stopped dead and pointed out the phenomenon to Musgrove. The man turned and looked. He shrugged.

'That's because it doesn't exist on this time-plane.' He stood with Wentik looking back across the plain.

'Odd feeling, isn't it?' he said surprisingly.

Wentik, who was aware of an overwhelming sense of displacement and helplessness, could only agree.

'Look, Musgrove,' he said in a voice trembling with a mixture of sudden anger and confusion.' What the hell's going on?'

'You want me to tell you?'

'Don't you think it's about time?'

'Probably – Let's go on, and I'll tell you as we walk.'

Wentik put the canteen of water on the ground, and sat down next to it.

'No. I'm staying here until you tell me.'

The other man shrugged. 'Suits me. It'll give us a break anyway.'

'All I want to know,' said Wentik, 'is what this place is. Where it is, and why I've been brought here.'

Musgrove looked around. 'What do you want to know first?'

'What this place is.'

'I told you,' he said. ' It's called the Planalto District. We're in a part of Brazil called the Serra do Norte in the Mato Grosso.'

'Go on,' Wentik said. 'That much I'd worked out for myself. I'm more interested in what you said about a time-plane.'

'It's difficult to conceive,' said Musgrove. 'But if you can imagine a place existing at two different times, then that is this. Where we are now is the Planalto of AD 2189. Where we were somewhere over there,' he waved vaguely with his hand, 'was in 1989.'

'And by walking a few hundred yards we jumped two hundred years?'

Musgrove nodded.

'There's a displacement field which controls the balance between the two times. If you stand in 1989 and look over here as we did a few minutes ago the District has a distinct perimeter. In fact, that border is the extent of the field. Cross it, and you are immediately transferred to 2189. The field is still all around us, but the visible line created by the forest in the past is now no longer there.'

Wentik unscrewed the top of the canteen he had brought with him, and took a mouthful of the warm water.

'This field that you mention,' he said eventually. 'I take it that it's artificial.'

Musgrove looked at him shrewdly. 'That's right. But I don't think Astourde knows that. Anyway, as far as you are concerned, all you need to know is that the Planalto District was discovered by the CIA, and is being studied by the same. How you got involved, I think I'll leave to Astourde to explain.'

'How far from civilization are we?'

'It depends on what you mean by civilization,' Musgrove replied. 'This is still Brazil. You saw how far we drove from Porto Velho. That's the nearest town.'

He stood up, and put an arm through the strap of the duffel-bag.

'Come on,' he said.' We've a long way to walk.' Wentik stood up too, and lifted the canteen. They continued in the direction in which they'd been walking before they stopped, the sun lowering now towards the horizon to their left. The heat was no less than it had been before, and Wentik found himself looking round at the sky to try and see some cloud. Even the warm, sticky rain would be preferable to walking in this unshaded glare. As they went on he and Musgrove drank freely from the canteen, until the sun set.

As night fell, the temperature dropped sharply, and they crawled into the blankets. Wentik shifted restlessly for hours, trying to find a comfortable lying position in the hard stubble. Eventually, he drifted off into sleep.

Wentik awoke, and found he was alone.

Musgrove's blankets were lying empty beside him, but the canteen of water had disappeared. He stood up, and felt a cool wind blowing. The sun was up, but the temperature had not yet started to climb.

He gathered up the blankets and crammed them into the duffel-bag that Musgrove had carried.

He looked all around him.

In the brittle stubble it was impossible to detect a trail. He screwed up his eyes and peered again at the surrounding plain. Miles away, almost on the horizon, he could see a tiny black dot. With no other features apparent, Wentik made for it.

Hurrying, in an effort to reach his destination before the sun became too hot, he traversed the distance in two hours, but was perspiring freely when he reached it.

It was a windmill, standing alone on the great plain, its vanes turning slowly in the wind. It was built of wood, stained a dark black to preserve its boards which, Wentik could see as he drew near, were warped and sagging.

A large stone flew past his ear. Then another, farther away.

He stooped, trying to present as small a target as possible. A pebble flew sharply at him and struck him on the shoulder.

It was Musgrove. The man was crouching just behind the mill, scooping up stones and hurling them wildly at him.

Wentik reached into the duffel-bag, and unfolded one of the blankets. Holding it like a shield in front of him, he advanced on the man. As he approached, Musgrove jumped up, darted towards him, then scrambled away on his hands and knees. He was babbling like a monkey. He stopped about twenty yards away, and squatted on his haunches facing Wentik.

He screamed.

Like the unseen animals in the night-time jungle, Musgrove screamed.

Wentik, confused and frightened, backed away, unsure of what he should do.

'What's the matter, Musgrove?' he shouted.

'Keep away from me! You're no good. You and your kind!'

The man jumped to his feet and ran towards Wentik, pausing only to pick up another stone.

Wentik lifted his blanket, but the rock caught him painfully on his left hand. Musgrove hurtled past him, propelled by his momentum. As he rushed past Wentik he was hissing air through his teeth like a child making snake-noises. He ran on for several yards, but tripped and fell heavily on to the hard earth.

He lay still.

Nursing his hand, Wentik walked cautiously towards him, ready for any sudden movement. But Musgrove was unconscious when he reached him.

Still confused, Wentik walked away from the man, and sat in the shade of the mill. The canteen was there, and Wentik drank from it gratefully.

For about two hours he sat there, listening to the creak of the mill vanes overhead, and feeling the breeze on his back.

Then Musgrove came round, and Wentik jumped to his feet to forestall any violence.

But the man just shook his head, stood up, and dusted down his clothes. He walked over to Wentik, and grinned at him.

'That gave you a start, didn't it?' he said.

Wentik, keeping his distance, said: 'What was all that about, Musgrove?'

The man laughed. 'Just a little game. Don't be alarmed.'

He lifted the canteen, and drank from it deeply. Then he splashed water over his face and arms, and screwed the top down. He threw it to Wentik, who slung it over his shoulder again.

Musgrove squinted up at the sun, then stooped and picked up the bag of blankets.

'Let's go and find Astourde,' he said. 'He'll be at the jail by now.'

He pulled another compass from his pocket, glanced at the sun once again, then walked away from the mill. Wentik allowed him to walk twenty yards, then followed, keeping his distance.

Five

•

Light fell upon his closed eyes, and Wentik opened them. Instantly he closed them again, but it was already too late.

He was lying in his cell, and it was pitch dark. But above the metal door was a device which had provided Wentik with many long hours of speculation as to its mechanism and purpose.

Its effect was plain enough. It consisted of a high-powered light-source which projected a narrow beam of light into the cell. This beam was directed on to one of his eyes by the guards in the corridor outside, but from then it was able to follow him automatically wherever he moved. In the tiny confines of the cell there weren't many places he could move to.

The only possible way to get the beam from out of his eyes was to turn his head and face the far wall. If he did this, music would come screaming through a large speaker set high in one of the other walls. The music was fast, loud and discordant, as if two exceptionally harsh pieces in non-related keys were being played simultaneously.

When he turned back to the beam of light, the music continued until the beam had locked on again.

Wentik alternated between the two discomforts, sometimes gladly suffering the musical racket to rest his eyes for a time, on other occasions he would seek out the beam and look into it, to be away from the dreadful noise.

Closing his eyelids would not unlock the beam, but afforded a certain relief. After a long process of experiments, he had found that to sit on the hard bunk of his bed and face the opposite wall, so that the beam fell across the bridge of his nose and on to his right eye, was the ultimate compromise. The discomfort from the beam was minimized, yet whatever it was that he triggered by turning his head completely away did not bring the music crashing in.

He was in the cell for an average of about twelve hours in each day, and the beam was switched off for about half of this time. Occasionally, the guards would switch on the mechanism while he was asleep (as they had done this morning) and he would be awakened by either the persistent dazzle of the beam or by the music as he turned in his sleep to avoid the light.

In a reflex that was now almost automatic, Wentik swung his legs off the bunk, sat up, and turned his head to the side. The guards, evidently wise to this manoeuvre, had locked the beam on to his left eye.

Blast! He turned his head away from the light, and winced as the music howled into the tiny, metal-walled cell. He turned back to the light, and got the beam to fall on to his right eye. Then, with the utmost care, turned and faced the wall again. The music had stopped.

He groped under the bunk, pulled out the metal pot, and urinated into it from a sitting position. Already, this cell was beginning to smell. He would have to change it soon. Perhaps today.

There was a low, bass-register noise outside the door: the voices of the guards who stood outside his cell throughout the night. Wentik listened. The men spoke for about fifteen seconds, then he heard them walk slowly down the corridor and away from him. He was free again for another day.

But he shivered. Partly from the cold – and partly at the anticipation of yet another day's aimless wandering along the corridors of the jail. He was becoming lethargic in his movements, sluggish in his thinking. The deathful routine of life in the jail had quickly established itself, and even quicker was beginning to break him out of his old patterns of behaviour. The only variation to routine that he had was the interviews with Astourde, and even they were now establishing a pattern of their own.

From the outset, he had been disoriented by the jail.

When he arrived with Musgrove he had been struck by its

barrenness of design and colour; a huge black-and-grey cube standing in dereliction on the lonely, windswept plain. Parked in front of it was an army helicopter, painted a dark green with a red and white cross on its nose.

Musgrove had said: 'Go round the back,' and darted away and disappeared into the building.

Curiously, Wentik walked around the building, still clutching his half-empty canteen of water.

At the back of the jail he came across a tiny lawn surrounded by trees, and here he found Astourde. The man was standing on a box, attempting to drill the other men. Like some army from a comic opera they were marching with a terrible lack of discipline. Colliding with each other, losing step, swinging arms at random, they looked ludicrous. Astourde was shouting incoherently at them, swearing and spitting his orders in a frenzy that did nothing to reduce the confusion. Earnestly, the men marched backwards and forwards for nearly half an hour, while Wentik watched with amusement.

Then, losing interest as of accord, the men gave up. One of them offered cigarettes around, and they all moved away from Astourde towards the jail block.

Wentik walked slowly across to where Astourde was standing on his box, alone in the centre of the lawn.

Astourde looked down at him, irritated that he had been seen at a disadvantage.

'Undisciplined crowd,' he muttered. 'As you're here now you might as well find yourself a cell. They're not too uncomfortable.'

He stepped down from his box and walked away, leaving Wentik standing alone with the blanket folded over one arm, and the canteen in his other hand.

From there, the conditions under which Wentik existed had deteriorated steadily.

Things started slowly enough. He selected a cell in a corridor on the first floor. Although there were no windows in any of the cells, from the corridor he could see out across the plain in the direction from which he had walked. Directly beneath the windows was the helicopter, and over towards the horizon he could pick out the black shape of the windmill, diminished by distance. Sometimes the horizon was obscured by heat-haze, and when the rains swept across the plain visibility was reduced to a matter of feet.

He didn't see Astourde again for several days. He wandered through the jail during the hours of daylight, and soon came to know it intimately. As far as he could tell it was almost completely empty. He would find, while walking, several doors that were locked; some permanently so, and the rest locked and unlocked at random. It became clear to him after a while that there was a small part of the jail he was never getting to see, and that was presumably where Astourde, Musgrove and the other men had their quarters.

Gradually, he found that the areas he walked through were getting smaller and smaller. More doors were being locked. Finally, on about the eleventh day after arriving, he found he was confined to walking in the corridor that ran outside his cell.

Something else he found alarming, but in ways considerably more subtle, was a sudden increase in his dream-activity. Every night he experienced several dreams of startling clarity. Some were lyrical and some frightening, but all were connected with his recent experiences. Astourde appeared in them often, as did Musgrove. His wife and children were in one, being pursued through a vast building by a gang of men. In another, he and Astourde were facing one another with rifles, calmly shooting at each other yet neither scoring a hit. Wentik, never one for precise dream-recall, found this upsurge first of great interest but latterly of worry.

Very slowly, the incidence of dreaming began to reduce, until after about a fortnight he was experiencing only one a night that he could recall in any detail.

One day, Wentik was intrigued to see that some of the men were working on the helicopter. About five of them were doing something to the rotor-vanes, though exactly what was not obvious at first. The helicopter was of the type with rotor-tip turbines. It seemed the men were attempting to remove the rotors but evidently had no idea of how to go about it. For three days they puzzled over it with much shouting between themselves. Wentik watched with great amusement from his corridor windows.

Then one morning he found that during the night immovable

steel blinds had been screwed across the windows the length of the corridor, and this small diversion was taken away from him.

By degrees, his tiny privileges were restricted. At first he had been allowed to collect his meals from the crude kitchen in the basement, but after he was confined to the corridor food was brought to him twice a day. Every day that passed brought smaller portions, and after a week at the jail, Wentik was accustomed to hunger being a part of his normal life. He was allowed to shave with an electric razor but no mirror, and was given water in which to wash every third day. There was no artificial regulation of temperature in the building and during the day the cells and corridor were stifling. At night, the temperature dropped sharply and he found it difficult to sleep.

With the constant lack of contact with anyone but the guards (who appeared to have been given instructions not to speak to him), the dwindling rations, and the constant discomforts of the jail, Wentik found his resistance was beginning to weaken. He could feel himself being stripped layer by layer of his own will, realizing that the implacability of his surroundings and the privations that were being forced upon him could break his whole identity if that were Astourde's intention. For the man had taken on the role of a hidden persecutor, whose very absence was an intimidation.

On the seventeenth day, Wentik was woken roughly by two guards who burst into his cell, and was dragged bodily down the corridor.

Unheeding of his protests, the guards hauled him down some rough stone steps, and out into the open. About three hundred yards from the jail there was a crudely built shack where all the men, with the exception of Astourde and Musgrove, stood outside carrying rifles. Wentik was thrown inside through a door, and found himself in total darkness.

For hours he had crawled inside the hut, finding that it was constructed of what seemed to be an endless maze of low-ceilinged tunnels, while outside the men fired blank cartridges into the air. When finally he had found a way back into the open air, he was thrown inside once again.

At the end of the second period inside he was dragged back to his cell and left there.

The day following this he was taken outside the jail again, but this time to a plot of bare soil some distance from the shack. Here he was given a long metal pole and a face-shield, and told to explode five land-mines that had been buried in the soil.

The guards stood round the perimeter and loaded their rifles with live ammunition. Wentik, still severely shaken by his experience in the shack the day before, hesitantly complied.

It took him an hour to find the first mine. He moved methodically and patiently, jabbing nervously at the soil with the pole, then taking a step forward. When the mine blew, a great spout of soil and pebbles gushed upwards with a roar that sickened him with its abruptness. Blown backwards by the blast and deafened by it, but otherwise unharmed, Wentik had difficulty in regaining his balance before moving on.

An hour and a half elapsed before he found the next. When the blast of flame and soil erupted, only six feet from him, he fell backwards with his heart racing and his breath tearing through his throat.

The next two came fairly rapidly one after the other, but by then he had control of himself.

The fifth mine ...

For three more hours he poked and prodded his way across the soil, and every minute that passed made the anticipation of the coming blast more dreadful.

Heavy rain fell while he searched, turning the soil to a sticky mud that clung to his shoes. Now his searching became desperate and he moved faster, knowing that it was only a question of chance whether he detonated it with the pole or with his foot.

Then one of the guards stepped across the mud, and took away the face-shield. There were only four mines, he said. The fifth one wasn't there.

The next, day, the nineteenth after his arrival, he had met Astourde again.

Left alone, he spent part of the morning wandering along the corridor outside his cell, trying to fit some semblance of logic to what was happening to him. He had come across a door which had been previously locked, discovered a staircase going up behind it, and had found a small room on the next floor.

Inside, Astourde sat at a desk. And the interrogation had begun.

That night, the pencil-beam of light and the ghastly music had been used for the first time. Although Wentik had twice changed his cell since, the beam-mechanism had either been moved to follow him, or was part of the standard equipment of each cell.

He had often wondered how the beam of light was able to follow his eyes so precisely, and as he sat there with it falling across the bridge of his nose the only explanation he could offer himself was that somehow the source was sensitive to reflections from his own retina, though the precision with which the beam followed him made him doubt even this.

So now the usual daily choice faced him. The discomforts of the cell, or the boredom of the corridor. He chose the latter, as he had done for nearly thirty days.

He got up from the bunk, and walked the two paces to the door, the beam of light faithfully dogging his right eye. He pushed the door open and put his head around it. There was no sign of the guards. He looked up and down the corridor; sunlight outlined bright squares around the shuttered windows.

He walked down the corridor, trying as usual the bolts on the blinds. It would mean a lot to him now if he could look out of the windows once again. But, as always, they were secure.

As he passed the door leading to the stairs that led to Astourde's office he did his daily mental coin-tossing. Boredom along the corridor, or the interrogation? Perhaps Astourde was already up there. He was often there early, knowing that Wentik would eventually prefer even the questioning to the loneliness here.

What made the choice so marginal was that the interrogation itself was a travesty. In a ludicrous attempt to intimidate Wentik, Astourde had fitted out the room with hard wooden chairs, bright lamps, and possessed an assortment of hypnotic devices whose correct use he evidently did not know. What made it even more laughable was that the apparent intent of the interrogation was to impress Wentik rather than to frighten him, as if Astourde was himself unsure of the potency of his position. The only really intimidating gesture was the presence of an armed guard in the room, but on the several occasions when Wentik had grown tired of the man's company and had walked away, the guard had done nothing to stop him.

He reached the end of the corridor, and pushed against the metal bars of the door there. It was locked. He turned, and walked back down the corridor, past his cell, to the first corner of the jail. Between here and the next corner, the one at the north-east of the jail, were three doors. He reached the first one, and it was open. So were the other two.

He walked to the corner, turned it, and found himself looking down the flight of stone steps with which his shins had made such close acquaintance the day he had been dragged out to the hut.

Cautiously he walked down the steps, and stopped at the bottom.

To his left was a lightly constructed wooden door. It was un-catched, and unlocked. Like the windows in the corridor its perimeter was limned with four dazzling lines of sunlight.

Wentik paused.

Was this a way out of the jail? No one seemed to be around, but he looked along the passage he was now standing in, half-expecting to see two of Astourde's men standing in the shadows.

The day before, during the short interrogation session, Astourde had seemed nervous and frustrated. The questions had been more pointless and repetitive than ever before, and Wentik had left after only a few minutes. Since then, he had seen no one except the two guards who had brought him food in the evening.

He looked at the door again, and pressed the palm of his hand against it. The wood was warm, and moved easily under the pressure. He pushed and walked through.

The sunshine was blinding.

Wentik, dazzled by the brilliance of the light after so many days in the gloomy corridors, sneezed dryly and painfully, and fell to his knees.

*

'Stand up, Doctor Wentik. I have some questions to ask you.'

Wentik looked up at Astourde, who was standing before him, his head coronaed by the sunlight. Wentik's eyes were streaming, and he sneezed again.

Astourde looked across at a group of men standing some distance away in white coats, and beckoned to them.

As the men approached, Astourde moved away and Wentik looked through his watering eyes at his surroundings.

He was crouching on the edge of a small lawn surrounded by tall beech trees. He remembered it as the lawn where he'd first seen Astourde on his arrival at the jail. He hadn't taken much notice then of the layout, but he was struck most of all now by the incongruity of its presence at the jail.

The sky was a brilliant shiny blue, and the sun was white and hot. Long delicate vapour-trails divided the blue, but there were no other clouds. His shadow on the grass was clearly etched by the undiffused sun.

Winged squirrels soared screaming from one tree to another, and a cloud of insects hovered beneath a branch of one of the largest trees. In the centre of the lawn was a wooden table with two chairs standing on opposite sides.

He looked behind him, and saw the high concrete face of the jail. The door through which he'd stumbled had closed, and a face now stared at him through a dust-covered window not far from it.

The two white-coated men grabbed him by the arms, and dragged him across the lawn towards the table. They walked quickly, not allowing him to regain his footing. He wondered why they were wearing white coats, and it occurred to him that they might be scientists conducting some kind of test on him.

Astourde was already sitting at one of the chairs, and the two men threw Wentik into the other; a cane chair which sagged uncomfortably under his weight.

The two men left him there, and walked back to the others. Wentik watched them. They were standing in the shade of one of the trees and as the two rejoined the others they all laughed loudly.

Wentik sat up, and lolled back in the chair, nearly causing it to collapse backwards.

The sun was shining, and it was too hot. There were a lot of insects everywhere, and the screaming of the squirrels was unpleasant.

And across the table sat Astourde, as patient as ever.

Reason returned to Wentik with a chill that momentarily took away the heat of the sun. He was still a prisoner after all, and he was going to be interrogated. (Was it a subtle diversion to further disorient him?) Perhaps in his tireless innocence he was forming what Astourde considered to be a solid block against the earlier questioning.

Astourde said: 'Tell me your name, Doctor Wentik.'

The same pointless questions as ever. Astourde stared blandly at Wentik, and smiled. Wentik looked back across the table.

Astourde was in his plain grey uniform. Both of his hands were resting on the top of the table. His smile broadened, and a sense of horror struck Wentik.

There were three hands on the table.

He stared . . . and Astourde's smile grew wider, and the scientists laughed, and a squirrel screamed.

A hand was growing from the centre of the table. Not resting there, like Astourde's, but *growing.* Wentik could see where it joined the smooth wood.

It was pointing at him.

Six

•

'Your name, Doctor Wentik. Give me your name.' Astourde's voice was insistent.

High in the sky, somewhere far above the tiny square of grass, a jet aircraft roared. Behind Astourde's head, away over towards the horizon, a small hill rose above the level of the plain. Halfway up the side, Wentik could see a metal mast, rising to a height of some three hundred feet above the plain.

He looked again at the hand growing from the table.

It was built with perfection, like a Greek carving in skin and flesh. It was the normal size of a man's hand, pale in the sunlight, but not bloodless. Tiny blond hairs grew on its back, refracting the sunlight. About three inches of wrist were visible before the arm disappeared into the tabletop, fusing into the grainy, dark-stained wood.

Incredibly, the hand started to drum its fingers, like those of a man kept waiting for an appointment.

'Your name!'

He took a breath. 'My name is Elias Wentik.'

The hand stopped its drumming, and relaxed on the table.

'You've committed a crime. What is it?'

'I—'

He hesitated. His first instinct was to think: *But there is no crime. I'm innocent—* But he and Astourde had gone over this a dozen times already. There was more to it than a mere protestation of innocence.

The hand was pointing at him again.

'I have not committed any crimes, as you well know.'

The hand didn't move. Steadily, it pointed straight at his heart.

Astourde slammed his own right hand against the tabletop, and started to rise. Wentik found his pulse beating noticeably in his temple.

'No crimes, Doctor Wentik? Your guilt is beyond doubt, yet you have committed no crimes! Now the truth!'

In the centre of the table, the rooted hand started stabbing in the air towards him.

Sitting down again, Astourde said: 'You see, I have no doubt myself that you are guilty. All I require is an admission from you.'

Wentik nodded.

'Now let us start again from the beginning,' said Astourde, an edge of triumph in his voice. 'What were you doing at the Concentration?'

Wentik ignored him. He was fascinated by the hand. It seemed to act entirely of its own will, disconnected from any apparent external control. The psychological impact it made had been negated, ironically enough, by Astourde. Now his interest in it was a scientific or engineering one. How did the thing work?

He pushed his chair back, and dropped to his hands and knees. The grass was warm to the touch, bringing a poignant flash of memory of the times when he and his wife had stretched for hours on the lawns of the college in their last term. In seconds the memory passed: it was part of the world now lost to him.

He crawled beneath the table, and looked up at the underside of the top surface. It was completely plain, giving no clue to the mechanism of the hand. Astourde's legs, protruding under the table, were wide apart and clad in badly fitting army trousers. Up near the man's crotch Wentik could see a tiny gap in the seam, pulled apart by the strain of the man's posture.

He crawled out again, and stood behind Astourde. The man was motionless, scarcely seeming even to breathe. On the table, the hand continued to stab the air in the direction of his empty seat.

The men standing in the trees were watching him carefully. Two of them were writing quickly on clipboards, and another was holding some kind of stopwatch.

Experimentally, Wentik walked directly away from the table, parallel to the high wall of the building.

At the edge of the grass there was a narrow strip of bare soil before the line of trees. As he walked beneath two of the large beeches, Wentik noticed that he had disturbed a colony of ants. As he passed, thousands of tiny insects ran aimlessly about.

Beyond the trees, the stubble began, stretching as far as he could see. Once clear of the shade from the trees he was immediately aware of the full heat of the sun. There was no shade anywhere, and as he stepped between the prickly clumps of stubble he accepted that there would be no escape for him across the endless plain.

He turned and sat down, facing back towards the lawn. The men in the white coats had left the comfort of the shade and were walking slowly towards him across the stubble. The only expression on their faces that Wentik could detect was one of slight annoyance.

Perhaps he shouldn't have disturbed them.

When he awoke the following morning, Wentik was interested to find that the beam of light was not in use. He lay on his bunk for about an hour, enjoying the relative luxury of being left alone, and coming back to full consciousness in his own time. This in spite of the hardness of the bunk, which was little more than planks of wood covered with a thin layer of foam rubber or plastic. He was still using the solitary blanket he had had since entering the Planalto District, but had managed to find some old sheets of rough cloth which he used as a pillow. His possessions which had been inside a suitcase on the lorry had never turned up. The men appeared to have left the lorry behind, as he had seen no trace of it while he had been at the jail.

When finally he did go out into the corridor, he discovered that no guards were anywhere in sight. For twenty minutes he roamed along the empty corridors, and was intrigued to find that a great many more doors were left unlocked than had been for some considerable time. Who, he wondered, was responsible for this? When he had determined that virtually half the jail was unrestricted he went down to the basement and opened himself a can of meat.

Tasteless and full of gristle, it repulsed him, but it was all there was. He was accustomed to this kind of food now.

When he had eaten, he went back up to the ground floor, curious to see what Astourde's new device had in store for him.

Astourde was sitting patiently at the table again, his narrow face as expressionless as ever.

'Sit down, Doctor Wentik,' he said as soon as he saw him.

Wentik walked to the table, noting that the hand still grew from its centre. It was motionless, its fingers resting limply on the surface of the table.

As he reached the table, Wentik stopped and looked around. He and Astourde appeared to be alone. There was no sign of the other men.

The previous day, Wentik's impressions of the garden had been distorted by the abrupt change in his environment. From the claustrophobic confines of his cell and the gloomy, ill-lit corridors, to the bright sunshine and colours of the lawn. There was something of the aspect of a dream in the impressions he still carried from the day before, however much he had tried to rationalize them.

So before he sat down at the table, he looked around. Everything was as before: the grass of the lawn, the wall of the jail forming one side and the beech trees forming three sides of the garden, and the undulating plain stretching to the horizon. Over there the wooden shack containing the maze, and next to it, the minefield.

Only Astourde sat at the table, and the hand still grew. Wentik sat down.

He stared at the hand, and thought: *My name is Clive Astourde.*

Astourde sitting opposite him saw his concentration, and shifted in his seat. The hand trembled slightly, then pointed at him.

Coincidence?

Wentik thought again: *I am a free man.* No change, the hand continued to point at him.

I am a prisoner, and my name is Elias Wentik of London, England.

Astourde, now moving uneasily, as if aware that he was no longer as much in control of Wentik as before, fiddled with his fingers on the edge of the table. As he did so, the hand drooped and returned to its former position.

It had seemed to Wentik the day before that the movement of the hand was in some way connected with his own thoughts. But the more probable explanation was that Astourde was able to manipulate it in some way.

Astourde cleared his throat. 'Who employs you, Doctor Wentik?'

Wentik watched the hand. He thought: *I am a civilian scientist,* and it stayed stationary.

'I am a Captain in the US Marine Corps,' he said blandly.

Astourde looked bewildered. The hand pointed at Wentik, then subsided. Then it pointed at him again.

'What—' Astourde stopped, then tried again. 'What were you doing at the Concentration?'

Wentik said: 'I was a prisoner.'

'What nationality are you?'

'I don't know.'

'Who am I?'

Wentik stared at the man. 'You are my interrogator.' The hand started stabbing the air towards him, and Astourde stood up.

'Your interrogator, am I?'

He pushed his chair aside contemptuously and walked over to the wall of the jail where his wooden box had been placed. He climbed on top of it and faced the lawn.

From behind the trees fringing the lawn stepped the other men. Ignoring Wentik, who sat at the table watching the proceedings with fascination, they walked towards Astourde and stood around him in an untidy bunch.

Wentik began to laugh, and went back unnoticed to his cell.

Wentik's life at the jail in the next few days became more or less centred around the hand, and the spurious psychological effect it had upon him. His early feelings of mild curiosity and timid acceptance of it soon gave way to an actively academic interest in its mechanism. Several times he crawled under the table during the interrogation sessions, but he was unable to satisfactorily understand its workings. Finally, he was forced to the conclusion that it was not an invention of Astourde's (nor indeed of any of the other men), but that he and his men had come across it when they first occupied the jail.

Once he accepted this his curiosity faded and he became more preoccupied with Astourde's irrational behaviour.

His motivations were completely obscured to Wentik, who could only puzzle over the inconsistency of the man's reactions. At times when Wentik tried to outmanoeuvre the hand on the table, Astourde's expression became troubled, and almost persecuted. But when he became less aggressive in his replies, Astourde would take the initiative and fire faster and faster questions. On one occasion, when Wentik had reached the stage where the interrogations were as tiresome as the earlier ones had been, Astourde had risen to his feet and started bellowing at him, the hand in the centre rigidly pointing. Then, Wentik had become genuinely afraid, and when the white-coated men began closing in on him, at some unnoticed signal from Astourde, he had retreated quickly to the relative safety of his cell.

Thus equipped with an acceptable working theory about the nature of the hand, but with a mounting awareness of Astourde's unpredictable behaviour, Wentik found that the dreams which were still troubling him began to fade, and within a few days occurred no more.

Thirteen days after he first encountered the hand on the table, Wentik was strolling down the corridor on his way to a makeshift breakfast in the kitchen when he noticed that the windows overlooking the plain had been unshuttered.

Outside the jail, the helicopter was still parked. But, Wentik noticed, the rotor vanes had at last been successfully removed, and were nowhere in sight.

When he reached the lawn, Wentik did not go straight to the table, but instead walked over to where the other men were standing. They appeared startled that he should approach them directly, and several of them backed away or moved around so that trees were between Wentik and them.

He went up to the nearest, a man with short black hair greased down over his skull. He looked apprehensively at Wentik.

'Who are you?' Wentik said direcdy.

'Me? I'm Johns. Corporal Allen Johns, sir.' He pointed to the others. 'And there's Wilkes, and that's Mesker, and Wallis and ... '

Wentik moved away, around and behind the men.

Idly, he picked up one of the clipboards lying on the ground. The sheet of paper had been divided into two broad margins, headed REACTIVE and PROGRESSIVE. Several tiny equations were scribbled across the page, regardless of columns, like absent-minded doodles. At the bottom, in the PROGRESSIVE column, someone had written:

Astourde
Wentik
Astourde
Musgrove (?)

The third name had been heavily underlined.

The man whose name was Johns said suddenly: 'Why don't you just stop resisting him, sir?'

Wentik, still puzzling over the meaning of the notes, said abstractedly: 'Who? Astourde?'

'Of course. We can all go back then.'

Not understanding, Wentik moved away from the group of men and walked to the nearest corner of the lawn. He sat down in the shelter of one of the beech trees, and studied the hieroglyphics on the clipboard. Johns followed him over and squatted beside him. Above their heads a squirrel suddenly leaped across the lawn, startling them both.

Its scream hovered in the confined space.

Wentik looked across the lawn at the table, where Astourde was still sitting. The man was gazing blankly at the hand in the centre.

Wentik said: 'What does Astourde hope to achieve with his questions? They're the same, over and over. It no longer even matters how I answer them.

Johns glanced at him shrewdly.

'Maybe that's the fault of the questioner rather than the questions.'

'Meaning ...?'

The man stood up and turned away.

'I don't know.' He thrust his hand into the pocket of his white coat, and laughed to himself. 'We're supposed to copy down all your answers, and give them to Musgrove. We used to joke about it at night, about what he does with them.'

'Musgrove?' Wentik said with a sudden interest. 'Where is he?'

'In one of the cells, I think.'

'You *think*?'

'I haven't seen him for some time. I think he's still here. We don't bother to take our notes to him any more.'

Johns walked away, leaving Wentik holding the clipboard. He looked at it again, but could get no sense from it. Finally, he dropped it on the soil and looked across at the other men.

Johns had rejoined the group, and some of them were watching him casually, almost as if he were of secondary importance to something which had yet to happen.

Astourde sat alone at the table in the centre of the lawn.

Patiently, Wentik sat beneath his tree, waiting to see what would happen. The sun was hot again, causing the horizon to waver, but over to the south-east clouds were greying the sky.

Nobody moved, though occasionally he would see someone pass a window in the jail-block. The silence was deep, broken only once by a jet aircraft crossing the sky at great height and speed.

On a sudden impulse, Wentik jumped up and sprinted across the lawn towards the jail. Someone had moved past the window near the light wooden door.

He kicked the door open, and found a surprised guard walking slowly down the corridor. He leaped on to the guard's back, and crooked his arm in a strangling hold across the man's throat. The guard threw up his arms in an attempt at self-defence, but Wentik had him in an unbreakable hold.

He dragged him to the floor.

Satisfied that the man could not escape, Wentik relaxed his grip slightly so he could speak. 'What's your name?' he said into the man's ear.

'Adams, sir. Don't grip me like that. I can't breathe.'

'OK. But I want information. Where the hell is this?'

'We're in the Planalto District.'

'What do you mean? Be specific' He tightened his hold again.

The man wriggled, then said: 'We're in Brazil. I was ordered here. Don't victimize me! It was Astourde … '

Wentik increased the pressure, and the man stopped. He hung in Wentik's arms, mouth open and gasping for breath. Taking advantage of the fact that the man was no longer struggling, Wentik dragged him into the nearest cell and laid him on the bunk.

'Now tell me slowly.'

The guard took a breath, and started to talk. He was just an ordinary soldier, he said. There'd been some trouble with him in his unit in West Germany, some scrap over a woman, and he'd been assigned to a special unit in the Philippines. The next thing he'd known he was flown to Rio de Janeiro with Astourde, and finally brought to the jail. As far as he was aware it was some kind of punishment. No one would tell him. He just did what he was told. It wasn't …

Wentik left him, and walked back on to the lawn. The sun, now approaching its zenith, hurt his eyes with its glare. He stood by the door and looked around the square of grass.

He thought of Musgrove, in a cell somewhere in the jail. And Astourde bound rigidly by the routine of interrogation. And he thought of the other men: the guards and these men who wore white coats. All of them appeared to go through a routine as meaningless to them as it was to Wentik.

When there is no escape from a prison, who are the prisoners?

He walked over to the table.

Astourde was still in his chair. He looked up as Wentik approached. 'Sit down, Doctor Wentik,' he said.

Instead, Wentik continued to walk around the table. In the centre, the hand rested idly, aimed in the general direction of his empty chair. Looking for a moment at the trees, he noticed that the men were alert, as if his movements were once again of major interest.

Suddenly, he seized the table and swivelled it round so that the hand pointed at Astourde. 'Why am I here, Astourde? Tell me!'

He jumped up in front of the man, waving a threatening fist. In the centre of the table, the hand had snapped to rigidity and was pointing.

Astourde fell backwards from his chair, and rolled on the grass. He tried to squirm away but Wentik, still gripping the edge of the table, turned it again so the aim of the hand followed the man. It began to stab the air.

Astourde shouted: 'Don't point that at me!'

He crawled away towards the group of men. Wentik dropped the table and ran after him. He caught him, and dragged him to his feet.

'Why have you been interrogating me?' he demanded. Astourde stared at him.

'To get the truth out of you! But that's finished now.'

He pulled himself free of Wentik's grip, ran through the cluster of men and started across the plain. Without slowing, he ran until he reached the shack and disappeared inside.

The man called Johns walked over to Wentik and said: 'You should have done that a lot earlier.'

He went to the table and righted it. In its centre, the hand was still stabbing blindly.

'Astourde relies too much on this device.' He ran his fingers along the edge of the table, hesitated over a particular point, and the hand relaxed again. 'While he was in control of this he felt he was the master of the situation.'

Wentik said: 'But he is blaming me for something I don't understand.'

'He told us that you brought us here.'

'No. He's responsible for everyone being here.'

Johns started to unbutton his white coat.

'It was something Musgrove said. About your research at the Concentration, whatever that is.'

'My work?' Wentik said, incredulously.

'I don't know anything about that.' He walked away from Wentik towards the shack, taking off his white coat and picking up a rifle from a pile of them by the edge of the lawn. Wentik followed him, noticing that underneath the coat Johns was wearing the uniform of the guards. The other men, too, had taken off their coats and were walking across the stubble.

He went to the pile of discarded coats, and picked one up.

'May I put this on?' he called.

There was no reply, so he pulled it across his shoulders and slipped his arms down the sleeves. On the ground he found a discarded clipboard and picked that up too. The paper was blank.

He sat in the shade of the trees for an hour, watching the unmoving face of the jail.

At the end of the hour the men standing round the shack shouted with delight, and blank cartridges rattled into the air. Occasionally, a man would scream, his voice muffled by the thin walls of the shack.

Much later, in the undiminishing heat of the long afternoon, Wentik found a rifle and some blank ammunition by one of the trees, and strolled across the plain to the others at the shack.

Seven

•

When Wentik awoke the following morning, he became immediately aware of a high-pitched mechanical screaming that rose and fell monotonously. He climbed off his bunk, pulled on his trousers and went out into the corridor. Here the sound was much louder.

He peered through one of the windows, screwing his eyes up against the early morning light. There was a shallow layer of cloud across the sky, and although the sun was not visible, already its presence was being felt. Wentik could feel the first traces of perspiration in the palms of his hands.

A thin mist of smoke surrounded the helicopter, and Wentik could just make out the shape of a figure inside the cockpit.

He walked along the corridors until he came to the main staircase, and went down. He went straight to the kitchen and helped himself to food. All this time he saw no one. He washed his face and hands under the cold-water tap and wiped them on the coarse material of the white coat. When he had finished, he put it on, and went to investigate the source of the noise.

He climbed the stairs to the ground floor, and walked along the central passage until he came to a door leading into a tunnel which ran from the main gate of the jail into a tiny exercise-yard in the centre.

There was silence now, and Wentik looked at the huge gate, held in place by a simple arrangement of wooden hasps. He lifted the two bars out of place, let them swing to the floor and pushed the heavy door open. He walked through into the open air.

About fifty yards away stood the helicopter, its nose facing him.

The vertical red cross on its white background was prominent in the drab colours of the surroundings. A man was standing by the machine, his head inside a large inspection-hatch on the side of the forward fuselage.

It was Musgrove.

Wentik shouted: 'Hey, Musgrove!'

The man looked up in surprise and saw him. He stepped backwards, slammed down the inspection panel, and hauled himself up into the large entry-hatch. He disappeared from view inside the machine, and reappeared in the perspex bubble of the cockpit. Falling hastily into one of the seats he reached up to the ceiling of the cockpit and depressed a lever. At once, the mechanical shrieking rose again, and the rotorless spindle at the top of the machine turned furiously. The stabilizing propellor on the tail started rotating. The noise grew higher in pitch, and smoke shot out of a line of exhausts in the base of the machine.

Wentik reached the helicopter, jumped up into it and climbed into the cockpit.

'What the hell are you doing?' he shouted at Musgrove.

The man looked over his shoulder frantically, and tightened his hold on the starter-lever. The high pitch of the motor continued.

'Keep away!' he yelled back.' I'm about to take off!'

'Not without vanes you're not,' Wentik shouted. 'For God's sake let go of that lever.'

The noise in the cockpit was deafening.

Wentik was vaguely familiar with the type of helicopter. During one of his industrial training periods several years before, he'd been attached to a British company that was assembling these machines under licence. He'd been shown over one once, or a type not too dissimilar to this, which was probably a slight advancement on the type he'd seen. The lever Musgrove had his hand on was the auxiliary piston starter; even if the helicopter had been fitted with its vanes it wouldn't have been able to take off. The main drive was from the rotor-tip jets, supplied from a main compressor housed inside the machine itself.

He grabbed Musgrove's arm and pulled. The man clung on

desperately, until Wentik dug his nails into his biceps. As Musgrove let go, the shriek of the starter-motor died away.

Musgrove clambered to his feet, and grabbed wildly at Wentik's neck. Blundering, his foot fell against the open door of a storage locker and he staggered forward into the main compartment of the machine. Wentik ducked down behind him as he fell, and heaved him towards the hatch. The man tripped on the lip of the hatch and dropped down on to the stubble, his head near one of the wheels.

Wentik squatted on the edge of the hatch, and looked down at the man. Something about his murderous and irrational behaviour unnerved Wentik.

He turned and looked up at Wentik.

'Surprised you again, did it?'

Wentik regarded him carefully.

'I think you're ill, Musgrove.'

'Well maybe I am. But that's not my fault, is it?'

He stood up, dusting himself down with precisely the motions he'd used the other time at the mill, and walked away towards the jail. Suddenly, he broke into a run, and disappeared through the black wooden gate.

Wentik climbed back up into the pilot's seat, and rested his hands on the main controls. He looked at the array of dials and instruments on the dashboard. Although he himself held a private pilot's licence, having flown light aircraft for relaxation for several years, none of the controls made much sense to him. How long would it take to learn to fly one of these? he wondered. Perhaps one of the men here was a pilot.

From what he remembered, this kind of helicopter was used for personnel-carrying, or as an airborne ambulance. It was fast and manoeuvrable, although of a comparatively short range. Its ceiling was quite high, but above twelve thousand feet its handling, Wentik had been told, was clumsy.

He looked at the gauges, and noted that the tanks were full. Musgrove evidently knew enough about the machine to be able to refuel it, though his elementary mistake in trying to fly the helicopter without rotors was incomprehensible.

By a process of trial and error, Wentik found the ignition-switch, and turned it off. There was no point in allowing the batteries of the auxiliary to go flat; they had been abused enough already, and Wentik had plans to use the machine to escape from the jail as soon as possible.

He slammed the hatch, and went back to the building.

Later in the morning, after more prowling around the jail and finding that virtually all of the interconnecting doors were now unlocked, Wentik decided to make a complete break with the environment of the jail, and walked alone across the plain towards the mast on the nearby hill. .

He still wore his white coat, and as he walked he found a small hand-mirror in one of its pockets. He looked at the reflection of his face, realizing with a start that it was for the first time in several weeks, and saw himself with the objective scrutiny of a virtual stranger.

His hair had grown very long, and was blowing uncontrolled across his face. His widow's peak, once prominent when he'd swept his hair back and combed it down flat, had vanished under his new fringe and, Wentik was pleased to notice, the texture of the hair had improved considerably and was lighter in colour.

Instinctively, he made to sweep it back, but stopped. In letting it blow in an unruly fashion the rather bony features of his face were softened, making him seem younger.

In fact, Wentik thought as he looked at his face, it suited him.

This glimmer of vanity raised his spirits considerably.

He reached the bottom of the mast, and found he was already unpleasantly warm. The sunless heat was in some ways more uncomfortable than the sun itself, and in addition carried the threat of rain.

The mast was supported at the bottom on a single ball-socket. Four quarter-inch twisted-strand cables anchored it, but because of the slope of the hill on which it had been built the two more southerly ones had a pronounced sag in them. Running up the side of the mast was a ladder, enclosed every few inches by a metal ring about two feet in diameter.

Wentik looked around him. He wanted to survey the surrounding land and this had seemed to him to be an ideal way. Now he was faced with the reality of it, the climb began to daunt him.

He looked up the ladder, overawed by the height of the mast. At the top he could see a narrow platform enclosed by metal railings. At least when he reached the top he would have a place on which to stand. He buttoned his white jacket tighdy so that it would not flap in the breeze, and began the climb.

Strangely enough, the first twenty rungs were the worst. Wentik climbed at a steady pace, not pausing or looking any farther than the next rung. He had no particular aversion to heights, but this was a new experience to him. Through the sensitive skin of his hands he could feel the mast vibrating with each step he took.

At the top of the mast, when he finally reached it, Wentik sat down gratefully on the platform. He leaned against the railing and felt the coldness of the breeze on his back. He took off the white coat.

When he had recovered his breath and felt a little cooler, he stood up and looked out across the plain.

Dominating the view was the black bulk of the jail. Seen from this height and distance it looked ugly and old, the dirty concrete walls reflecting the light from the sky with a flatness of tone that Wentik found repellent. The roof was made of wood, painted or stained a streaky dark brown. At approximately twenty-yard intervals he could see abandoned sentry-boxes along the perimeter of the roof.

Looking to the south, Wentik tried to make out the edge of the plain, the Planalto District, instinctively feeling a greater sense of imprisonment from its bleak immensity than he had ever done while cooped up in the cells.

He felt a hopeless sensation of separation from reality. There was no way out. In all directions, the same depressing prospect of boundless plain presented itself to him. Only in the east was there any change in appearance of the plain. It looked as if darker vegetation grew there, though it could be an illusion caused by cloud-shadow. It was too far away to tell.

Wentik became aware of a slight vibration in the platform, and he gripped the thin tubular fencing that was all there was between him and a two-hundred-foot drop. He looked down through the wire-mesh of the platform and saw a grey-uniformed figure steadily climbing the perilous ladder.

Astourde? Why should he follow him up here?

His first thought was that the interrogation was to be resumed. Then he thought again; Astourde's withdrawal the day before had been complete. He no longer had the tacit or covert support of his men, and any new movement he made now would be on his own.

Wentik dismissed the thought.

He sat back again, and relaxed against the railing. He waited for Astourde to arrive.

Astourde heaved himself off the last rung, and sat heavily beside Wentik.

'Elias,' he said breathlessly. 'We've got to talk.'

Wentik winced. The ingratiating emphasis Astourde put on the 'Elias' jarred on him. He looked at the man.' What do you want?'

'The same as you, I suppose.'

He was breathing heavily, yet made no attempt to loosen the tunic of his uniform.

'I wish you hadn't followed me up here,' Wentik said pointedly. 'There's nothing more to say.'

'Yes there is.'

Astourde reached inside his tunic and pulled out a strip of translucent paper, now wrinkled and dirty. Inside, the single frame of colour film was still there.

He held it over the edge of the platform, and let it go.

'Things like that photograph of the jet. Reasons for our being here. What we're going to do next. I'm not sure.'

His hand returned to the inside pocket.

Wentik said: 'What are we going to do about getting away from this place?'

'I don't know. There's the helicopter, I suppose.'

Wentik looked at it, almost hidden by the bulk of the jail. Two men were working together near the tail-rotor.

'I caught Musgrove this morning. He was trying to take off in it.'

'Was he?' Astourde said sharply. 'I told him not to try.'

'Why were the rotors removed?' Wentik said.

Astourde fidgeted, his hand out of sight inside his tunic.

'I thought you might steal it.'

'So you knew I could fly?'

'Yes.'

Something had caught Wentik's eye as he looked at the helicopter. Somewhere along one of the walls of the jail facing him ... He screwed up his eyes in an effort to see it.

'Musgrove's been acting very strangely,' he said.

'Maybe.'

Astourde stood up, and leaned against the rail of the platform, looking away from the jail. While they had been talking the cloud-layer had thinned and now the sun was at its full noon heat. The plain shimmered with thermal currents.

Wentik stood up too, and looked at the jail.

There. About half-way along the wall he could see a light-coloured protuberance. In the brightness of the sun, the drab colouring of the walls had a deadening effect on the eyes. But now he had pinpointed it he could see it quite distincdy. It was coloured a pale buff, almost white. It had no shape Wentik could identify, yet its presence on the wall did not seem to be arbitrary. His curiosity aroused, Wentik wondered what it could be, placed with apparent deliberation on an otherwise blank external wall.

There must be some reason for it. Yet his curiosity persisted.

When he had time, perhaps later in the day, he'd have a look at it at closer quarters.

He caught Astourde's arm, to draw his attention to it, but the man resisted.

'Here,' he said. 'Look at the hut. I had to sleep there last night.'

Wentik looked down at the building, and noted with surprise its apparent smallness. On the occasion he'd been inside he had felt subjectively that the maze of tunnels inside was infinitely large. At the time he had been terrified, but looking at it now the paradox of its size intrigued him.

He felt a twinge of guilt. It had been his actions, after all, that had made Astourde go to the hut.

He said: 'About getting away from here—'

Astourde interrupted: 'I've got some maps, Elias. We could try to make for Porto Velho if you like. Or the coast. What do you think?'

'I don't know. I'd like to see the maps.'

'There's something else . . . '

'What?'

'I'm not sure,' Astourde said slowly. 'It's something to do with the reason you're here. Everything's changed now.'

'I don't understand.'

'After what happened yesterday. All that shooting, and when I was alone in the hut. I began to see things from your point of view. Then when I came out this morning, it was as if you didn't exist any more.'

The man took hold of the nearest metal ring around the ladder, and swung his leg on to the rung.

'What do you mean, Astourde?'

'Let's discuss this later.' He climbed down one more rung. ' It's too hot now. Wait until it's cooler. Come to my office tonight.'

His head disappeared from view. Wentik watched him through the floor, as he had watched him ascend. The man's movements were slow, meticulous, as if he had a motor inside that regulated his bodily co-ordination.

For whatever reason, his term of imprisonment seemed to be at an end. Astourde treated him now with virtual deference. Wentik could imagine the man in other surroundings, perhaps as an officious manager in some government department, supervising pay-office staff. Arrogant with his subordinates, servile to his superiors. But his day here had come, and gone.

Where, Wentik wondered, did he himself fit into Astourde's new plans? If the man had any.

Wentik leaned back against the rail, feeling the slight vibrations in the platform caused by Astourde's descent. The sun's rays fell on one side of his face, the other was tempered by the breeze. It was almost comfortable.

Every so often his gaze would wander to the eastern horizon, and he looked at the faint smudge of darker vegetation.

Eight

•

Astourde found Musgrove in the tiny exercise-yard in the centre of the jail. The man was standing to one side, looking up at the lines of barred windows in the opposite wall.

'I don't understand,' he said when he saw Astourde coming towards him. 'None of the cells has a window, yet if you look on the outside walls there are several.'

Astourde said: 'Don't bother about that. There's something I want you to do for me.'

Musgrove walked over to Astourde, and pulled open the door of a lean-to shed against the wall of the courtyard.

'What is it?'

Astourde watched as the man reached inside and lifted out the end of one of the helicopter's rotor-blades. Abruptly he changed the subject.

'I thought— Why did you hide those?'

'You told me to.'

'I didn't say hide them. I said to remove them.'

Astourde's face revealed his sudden anger and he turned his back on Musgrove as if remembering what had happened the day before.

'Wentik says he saw you at the helicopter this morning.' Musgrove let the end of the rotor rest on the floor, and he straightened.

'Yes. I caught him trying to take off in it. He admitted he was trying to escape.'

'*Wentik* was in the aircraft?'

'Yes.'

Musgrove stood before him sullenly. It seemed that his attitude now was a reaction against Astourde's own behaviour the day before. In the few months he'd known Musgrove he had often been reluctant to obey him, but to Astourde's knowledge he had never been told a deliberate lie.

He said to the man: 'Wentik says it was you trying to fly the machine.'

'Ha!' Musgrove threw back his head. 'Without rotors?'

'Yes. Without the rotors. What was the idea?'

A man came into the yard, walked over to Musgrove and gave him a metal box containing several wrenches and spanners. Without looking at Astourde, he walked away.

Astourde said: 'Hey, you!'

The man stopped, and turned round.

'What do you want?' Astourde said to him.

'I was looking for Mr Musgrove. I couldn't find him in the office, so—'

'All right.' Astourde turned back to Musgrove.' I want you to do something for me.'

The man looked back at him cautiously, as if expressing tacitly the lack of authority Astourde exerted over him.

'What?'

'You too,' Astourde said to the other man.' See if you can find any local inhabitants.'

Musgrove said: 'You mean travel on foot?'

'Yes. Take as much equipment as you want, and as many men.'

'And if I don't go?' Musgrove replied, with a hint of threat in his tone.

'I . . . don't know.' Astourde said: '*Will* you go?'

'All right.' Musgrove looked at the other man. 'But I'll go alone.'

'It's up to you.'

Astourde turned away, and headed for his office. With Musgrove out of the way he would feel more capable of dealing with Wentik.

In the late afternoon, Wentik returned to the jail and took more food. He saw no one, yet heard the occasional noise or movement coming from the floor above him.

During the interrogation his desire to leave the jail had been consciously kept at bay while he waited for positive developments. Now he was virtually free to do as he pleased, his yearning to get away from the jail, to get back into contact with the outer world, to continue his work and to see his family again ... all these became a major obsession. Yet, at the same time, he was rapidly coming to terms with the remoteness of the jail and already he was growing to accept his escape as a long-term proposition.

With this in mind, he determined to find out what he could about this place. He could perhaps even turn up some way of hastening the process.

When he had eaten, Wentik went out again to the small lawn at the rear of the prison. It was as quiet now as the rest of the building. The table at which he had been interrogated had been dragged over to the wall and it stood there in forlorn silence, its synthetic hand limp, and pointing dispiritedly towards the jail.

He looked at it wryly for a moment, remembering how its sinister surrealism had haunted him at first. He ran his fingers over its smooth lines, and was slightly alarmed to find that it was warm, evidently through lying in the sun. Nevertheless, the discovery disturbed him.

On the earlier occasions when he'd tried to find out how the thing worked, he'd been restricted by the presence of Astourde. He still had no real idea of how the controls worked, though there was evidently some fingertip control along the edge at the rear. Wentik bent down and looked along the edge.

At once, he saw a small metal plate set into the wood. On it were embossed the words:

Companhia Siderurgica Nacional
Volta Redonda
Poder Directo

He laid the palms of his hands on the top surface of the table and let his thumbs drop down, as Astourde had always done. He experimented for a moment or two, then found the right place. If he pressed down simultaneously with both hands a lever dropped down ... and the hand became rigid. Squeeze the lever, and the hand started the stabbing motion.

It fascinated him as it always had, moving backwards and forwards like the head of a swimming moorhen.

His hands on the table's surface could feel the vibration of the movement. He let go, and the hand stopped.

Satisfied, Wentik stepped back. It was just a gadget, after all, and anyone could work it.

He walked away from the table, across the lawn and out on to the plain. The sun was starting to lower in the sky, but sunset was still a couple of hours off. The temperature was high, probably well into the eighties.

He trudged purposively towards the shack.

Like the jail, it had an old and ramshackle appearance. Two of its walls were made of concrete, but the remainder were wooden. Wentik walked around it slowly.

When Astourde had left him at the top of the mast, he'd spent several minutes studying the shack from the advantage of height. It was asymmetrical, built originally in the shape of a cube, but later appendages had not followed any particular pattern. It sprawled untidily across the stubble, with many walls and angles, different roofs and cavities.

There were four entrances from the outside, and as he passed each one Wentik peered through it.

One of the openings was on the side of the shack at present facing the sun, and here Wentik could see farthest into the interior without actually entering.

The time he'd been thrown into the shack, he had been made unobservant by his fear. He'd attempted to work out its design, but had experienced a kind of intellectual withdrawal which had closed his mind to it, and let him react to it in an entirely emotional way. As he looked at it now, though, Wentik found he could inspect it analytically and with professional engineering insight.

The conditioning of human reflexes had formed part of his research, and he had published several papers on the uses of mazes in the training of unshaped minds.

Anyone thrown violently into this building, Wentik saw, would be instantly confused and disorientated. All surfaces, horizontal or vertical, were painted the same matt black. Although the corridor down which he was looking was no longer than seven feet, and the sun was shining more or less directly into it, the feeling of a greater length was very strong.

When a frightened man has no idea of where his next step may take him, a complete breakdown of normal mental processes can quickly follow.

Wentik's own experiences in the building had frightened him badly at the time, but he had recovered quickly afterwards. He knew, though, that if Astourde had had sufficient knowledge of interrogatory processes he would have put him back inside the maze the following day.

But once had been bad enough.

His memories of the incident were charged with nightmarish images of irrational fear and panic given full vent by the pitch dark inside the maze and the rifles being fired outside. Now he had an opportunity to rationalize his feelings, he could attribute scientific thought to what had happened.

At the end of the short corridor was a black-painted door, hinged on both its sides. Wentik scrambled down the corridor (the ceiling of it was low enough to cause most men to walk with their heads permanently bowed – another psychologically intimidating feature) and pressed his hands against it. He felt it start to give, moving with the right-hand hinge as the pivot, and opening to the left. He relaxed his pressure, and the door stopped moving.

The hinging was evidently some device which allowed the door to pivot on either side. He put his eye to the crack he had opened, but could see nothing. Behind the door it was totally black.

There would be no point in going farther. He couldn't make scientific observations in the dark. Wentik chuckled.

Intrigued by the building, he went back down the corridor and into the open air. He hurried back to the jail, and returned with a powerful torch which he managed to borrow from one of Astourde's men hanging around the exercise-yard.

Perspiring from the two-way walk across the hot stubble, he

clambered back down the corridor and looked again at the door. He pushed it, and it swung over to the right as he had known it would. It stopped with a muffled thud at an angle of about sixty degrees to its former position.

As it closed, it felt as though its movement were in some way spring-loaded.

Now, to the left, an extension of the tunnel had been exposed, branching off from the first at an angle. Wentik crawled down it.

After approximately another seven feet he came to a second door, and he stopped. He looked back, and could see sunlight filtering down the corridor behind him.

The door solidly blocked the tunnel before him as the other had done. He pressed his hands against it, and felt it give slightly – this time with the left-hand hinge as pivot.

Shining his torch all round, in an attempt to find out how it worked, Wentik pushed the door the whole way. As had happened before, after he moved the door a short distance, springs carried it the rest of the way and it shut with a feeling of solidity.

Now a tunnel to his right had been exposed.

Instead of moving down it he turned round and crawled back to the first door.

No longer did the sunlight shine through. The door had shut behind him, barring the whole corridor.

So ... The doors were interconnected. Once the next door had been opened, the one behind would close.

In other words, once the decision had been made to open the next door there was no way back.

Unless ... Wentik pressed his hands against the door and pushed. It swung to the right again and behind him the second door moved.

Now he was beginning to get confused. He steadied himself, realizing that he was getting into precisely the state of mind the designers of the maze had intended.

The first door had swung to his right, closing off the corridor which led to the outside and opening a new tunnel, one that he hadn't yet seen, which branched off to his left. He pressed against the door again, but now it was immovable.

The only way to open the door, it seemed, was from the corridor which at any one time was being blocked by it.

He scrambled back down to the second door, and found that it had moved in its turn and now exposed a corridor branching off to *its* left.

Wentik shone his torch to and fro, trying to see any structural gaps in the tunnels. He wanted to get outside and try to work it out objectively. Instead, he was trapped inside.

Steady. There was no trap. There was a way out, but he had to keep going forward to find it.

He sat back for a moment or two, trying to visualize the maze as it would be seen from above. If each door was triangularly hinged, and there were always three passages at each intersection, then that would mean that each tunnel described one-sixth of a regular hexagon. Further than this, to open the hatch blocking the corridor to the front would close the one behind, and possibly several more. Perhaps every door in the maze was linked to all the others, so that the movement of one would automatically trigger the movement of all the others.

Ingenious. But terrifying.

Sweat trickled from his armpit down the side of his chest. Impatiently he massaged it into the fabric of his shirt and looked around.

He crawled back to the door he thought of as the second one, and went through. At the end of the short corridor there was another one. He pushed it and went through ... the one behind moving and closing his route backwards. He reached the next one, went through. And the next one.

For half an hour he pressed on through the maze, occasionally pausing to inspect the construction of the tunnels. As far as he could tell from the sound produced by tapping the walls, they were built of light wood. His passage through the tunnels became progressively more unpleasant as the temperature climbed, and at times he felt the nudge of claustrophobia. As he went deeper into the maze he found that there was no regular pattern; some of the doors swung to the right, and some to the left. Sometimes doors were open already when he reached them, and he could pass straight through. Once he went through three successive doors without having to move one. At the end of this a door barred his way, he pushed it, and he heard all three doors behind him close.

When fright irresistibly grew in him it helped to remind himself that only a topologist could have designed and built this maze. His scientist's intellect finally recognized this, and the fear passed.

Quite unexpectedly he reached a door that resisted his pushes. At first alarmed, he put his weight against it, until it occurred to him to pull it.

It opened on to dazzling sunlight.

The final trick. A one-way door to the outside. A dazed man stumbling against it might turn back without considering, and return to the maze.

The sun was setting now, and its rays shone almost directly down the corridor.

Exhausted, Wentik crawled out on to the stubble and leaned back against the wooden wall of the shack.

He sat for a while without moving, grateful for the fresh air which although still warm was cooler than that inside the shack, and he wondered at the intelligence which had built the maze.

In some ways, the most startling thing about it was that there were four entrances to the maze. He remembered that the first time he had been inside it he had emerged at the same side of the building as that at which he had entered. Did that always hold true? he wondered.

If that were so, it meant that either there were four mazes entirely independent of each other, or, more probably, that there were four routes through, using the same passages. In spite of its ramshackle appearance and apparently haphazard construction, the maze-shack was a highly advanced weapon of torture.

His professional spirit roused, Wentik walked round to one of the other entrances and, disregarding his personal hardship, plunged inside once more.

When he re-emerged, three-quarters of an hour later, Astourde was waiting for him.

Nine

•

The two men walked back to the jail in silence. Night had fallen while Wentik was inside the maze, and now the air was cold.

They reached the jail-building, and Wentik allowed Astourde to lead the way up the narrow stairs towards his office; the room where the early interrogation sessions had taken place.

At the door, Astourde paused.

'Would you like some food, Elias?' he said. 'I've laid on a meal for you.'

Wentik, who was feeling a growing hunger, said: 'Where is it?'

'In here.'

Astourde pushed the door and held it open for Wentik, reaching in awkwardly and partially blocking the entrance. Wentik walked through.

The room was in darkness, except for the low table-lamp on the desk. The circle of light it threw fell mainly on to a hard wooden chair at the side of the desk. In the gloom, standing back from the table, were several of Astourde's men, wearing their white coats.

Behind him, Astourde softly closed the door, and turned a key. Wentik turned to face the man, who stood with his hands behind his back. His shoulders, which for the last twenty-four hours had been slumped, were now erect. The grey uniform looked military again, instead of being an uncomfortable and ill-fitting garment.

The aura of menace, that had so influenced Wentik in his early days at the jail, had returned.

'Sit down, Doctor Wentik,' Astourde said quietly. 'We haven't finished with you yet.'

Wentik looked round the room. The tableau was like a scene from a bad American detective film. After the mechanical sophistication of the maze, Astourde's idea of psychological intimidation, shorn of its surprise value, had the subtlety of a comic-strip. Anyway, Wentik was tired of these games. Astourde's dependence on setting and environment grew more transparent every day.

And the question of his authority over Wentik had been settled already. It took more than this to intimidate him now. He looked blankly at Astourde.

'No.'

Wentik could sense a growing tension in the room as he uttered the word. The men in the white coats, a troupe of bit-players, looked at Astourde as if for instructions.

The little man walked pompously to the desk, and sat down with ceremony, as if the other men in the room were awaiting his pleasure. He opened his mouth to say something.

Wentik said: 'Get out! The lot of you!'

Astourde leaped to his feet again.' Stay where you are!'

He glared at Wentik.

'Sit down!' he bellowed, as if volume were a substitute for authority. His face grew blotchy in the dim light from the table-lamp.

Wentik walked calmly to the door and turned the key which Astourde, through some oversight, had left in the lock. He opened it.

Turning to the men, he said in a firm voice: 'Ignore that man. He has no authority over you. Get out immediately.'

The man nearest to Wentik shrugged and walked out straight away. The other men looked at Astourde, then at Wentik, and moved to the door.

As they filed past him, Wentik looked at them closely, wondering where Musgrove was.

When the last man was out in the corridor Wentik shut the door, turned the key, and pocketed it.

'Forget them, Astourde,' he said. ' We were going to have a talk this evening, if you remember.'

He groped along the wall, and found a switch. The lights came on from a glass panel set into the ceiling. Wentik looked around the room, realizing that this was the first time he had been inside it without the oppressive feeling of imprisonment.

Astourde blinked.

'I'm— I'm sorry about that, Elias,' he said.

'Did you say you had some food?' Wentik said. The little scene had left him surprisingly unmoved, and his hunger was as sharp as before.

The man in the grey uniform (once again a bundle of clumsy clothes) opened a drawer in his desk, and took out a tray covered with a cloth. He removed it, and on the tray was a plate of stew.

'Help yourself,' he said dispiritedly. He stood up, and turned off the desk lamp. He moved about the room, letting his hands droop and swing against pieces of furniture.

Wentik sat down at the desk, and pulled the plate towards him. It was still hot, evidently having been prepared just before he came to the room. He looked at it with the uncritical eye of someone who hasn't eaten properly in weeks, and saw to his surprise that trouble had apparently been taken over its preparation. Everything must have come from cans, but thick chunks of meat were complemented by green beans, carrots and potatoes. He took a forkful, and ate it hungrily.

As he ate, he looked round the room curiously, seeing it now with the same detachment as he was finding with all other aspects of the building. It was surprisingly well furnished, compared with most other parts of the jail. Apart from the desk and two chairs there was a tall wooden cupboard in the corner. It was closed, but the padlock which held the door was hanging agape from the catch. The window was curtained with soft brown material. There were several filing-cabinets along the wall behind Astourde's seat, and a photograph hung in a frame on the wall.

Wentik studied it curiously.

The photograph was of the jail. It was taken from the front of the building, where the helicopter was presendy parked. In each of the sentry-boxes along the roof stood guards, who appeared to be unarmed. Above each box flew a flag. In front of the jail there stood an orderly parade of uniformed men, standing like soldiers in a perfect square. Before them, on a raised dais, stood a man in a uniform of evident high rank. At each side of him stood aides.

When Wentik had been in the room before, the photograph had not been there. Astourde must have concealed it from him, and now he began to understand why.

The scene in the photograph was remarkably similar to the one presented to him the day he arrived at the jail, when Astourde had been attempting to drill his men, unaware that Wentik had seen him. He realized that if he had been able to worry this weak spot of Astourde's at the time – the man had been obviously embarrassed about it – then his interrogation might never have started.

Breaking into his thoughts, Astourde suddenly said: 'I'm sorry about that.'

'You've already apologized.'

'I know. But I really am sorry. It was pointless.'

Wentik turned round to look at the man standing behind him, facing a blank part of the wall.

'What was the idea?'

'I'm not sure,' Astourde replied. 'I thought it might work again.'

'The interrogation?'

'Yes.'

'It didn't work before.'

Astourde turned round quickly. 'Oh yes it did.'

Wentik chewed more of his stew, and thought about that for a while. There was more he needed to know about Astourde's motivations before progressing. He ate his way through the rest of the meal, and pushed aside the cardboard plate.

'I'm ready,' he said.

Astourde walked around the desk, and switched the lamp back on again. Wentik suddenly realized the other man's dependence on gadgets, how all his movements centred around a particular object wherever he was. Removed from them, he was helpless.

The light from the lamp now illuminated most of the desk. Astourde sat beyond it, his face lit by the light reflected up from the surface of the desk, giving him a most unusual aspect.

'What do you want to know?'

Wentik said: 'Everything.'

'I don't know much myself,' Astourde said, in a voice carrying a warning hint of qualification.

'I daresay. But I want to know as much as you.'

'All right.'

Wentik held out his left hand, and counted off on his fingers.

'First I want to know who you work for. Second, why I was brought to this place, and on whose authority. Thirdly, what this place is and when we are going back.'

'Is that all?'

'It'll do for the moment.'

Astourde braced his feet against a strut under the desk, and leaned backwards so that his chair was at a precarious angle. Wentik watched him steadily. He and Musgrove – why did they act the way they did? Wentik had yet to see either of them perform a single rational or logical act, though their behaviour was always superficially of extreme simplicity. Another thing that worried him was their lack of consistency; nothing ever seemed to be carried through to its conclusion. And perhaps the most disturbing factor of all – his own relationship with Astourde, which maintained a shifting balance between aggressivity and passivity.

As he waited for Astourde to make some reply (the man was staring at the recessed lights in the ceiling in a ridiculous attitude of absorption) he was suddenly reminded of a man who had once worked under him at the chemical corporation where he had started his work in the States. This man had terrorized his own subordinates from the moment he arrived, yet when Wentik had finally dismissed him, the change in his manner to obsequity had been almost humorous.

'Elias, do you want me to tell you things I'm not able to?'

'What do you mean?'

Astourde said: 'I've been working under orders. They were written and sealed, and I had to destroy them shortly before I first met you.'

'You said you worked for the government. Are you in the army?'

'No.'

'Yet you wear a uniform, and have men who apparently act under your orders.'

'It was part of the idea. I thought a uniform would influence you more. So although you could say I'm a civilian, we work administratively from the Pentagon.'

'We?'

'The committee. I'm not on my own.'

'I'd worked that much out myself.' Rather than enlighten him, Astourde's remarks were beginning to confuse Wentik.

'Who is on this committee?'

Astourde said: 'Government scientists mostly. One or two generals from the Army and Air Force. It started out as a military operation, but then the government got wind of it, and it was centralized from Washington.'

'Go on.'

'The first time anyone became aware of the existence of the Planalto District,' Astourde said, 'was about eight months ago. A small seismological expedition came here to set up an automatic monitoring device. The whole expedition disappeared, and nothing has been heard from them since. After a few weeks had elapsed a second team was sent out in search, and they disappeared too. None of this was made public because there were Communist agents operating in Brazil. An army helicopter was sent next, and that also disappeared without trace.

'After this, a properly equipped investigation team was sent, making hourly reports back to a base camp near Porto Velho. After three weeks' search they came across what we now know as the Planalto District.'

'Where we are at present,' Wentik said.

Astourde nodded.

'It wasn't known at that time,' he went on, 'that there was an external factor involved. A vast, treeless plain in the centre of the Mato Grosso is unexpected enough. The fact that it was perfectly circular, down to almost the last inch, was something else again. The immediate conclusion, incidentally, was that it was some kind of weapons-range built in secret by a foreign power. Until you've tried to move about in the Mato Grosso, you don't know what communications are like round here.

'What we now know is that the District is created artificially by some kind of displacement field generator. There is also a directional alternator involved that switches the field on and off, in such a way that although it is possible to enter it merely by walking into it, it is impossible to leave it by the same means. This was tested stroboscopically, and it was found that the field pulsates at about a hundred cycles a second.'

Wentik said: 'Musgrove told me it was artificial.'

Astourde looked at him sharply. 'Musgrove . . . ?'

'He brought me here, Astourde. You haven't forgotten?'

'No. No. I wasn't sure how much he had told you.'

He told me that he didn't think you knew about the field, Wentik thought, looking at the man across the desk and remarking to himself again how much the man had changed in the short time he had known him.

Astourde went on: 'This was where I came into it. I was on the staff of one of the teams. We were observing the District for a period of about three weeks, when a man was suddenly seen wandering inside. His movements were erratic, as if he were unsure of direction, or as if he were looking for some landmark. Finally, he stopped about three hundred yards from us. We had moved around the perimeter to keep abreast of him. He spent several hours erecting some wooden signs, which he had been dragging earlier. He seemed to be totally unaware of us.'

Wentik said: 'Why didn't you attract his attention?'

'You think it wasn't tried? We shouted at him, flashed lights, even fired rifles into the air. But for some reason the sound didn't carry.'

'What was on the signs?'

Astourde opened a drawer of his desk, and brought out a spiral-bound notebook, which he laid before him.

'There were seven signs in all, and they read like this. On the first one the man had written: *My name is Pfc Brander, US Army. I don't know where I am, or what has happened.* The second read: *There are other men with me but I cannot say where they are now. I have been on my own for six days.*'

Wentik interrupted: 'How had he made these signs?'

Astourde shrugged.

'Pieces of old wood, I imagine. There's plenty of it lying around. All that we could tell from that distance was that he had boards on which he had painted the messages.'

Wentik nodded.

Looking back at his notebook, Astourde went on: 'The third one read: *Do not try to follow me. I cannot escape.* The fourth one: *I came in somewhere about here. If you can read this, do not follow me.* The fifth one: *There is a man here who has gone insane. I have nightmares every night. Two men have committed suicide*'

Astourde paused.

'When the man wrote this he was evidendy going through the symptoms of fear and confusion that, for some reason, attack everyone who comes into the Planalto District. All my men have had them, and there seems to be nothing we can do about them.'

Wentik said: 'You say that everyone has them?'

'You mean you don't?'

'I don't think so. I had some pretty vivid dreams for a week or so, but nothing else.'

'We thought not. Musgrove pointed it out to me.'

Wentik said: 'What was on the other signs?'

'The sixth one said: *This can only be somewhere in the future. I have seen a strange aircraft, and someone found a book. I'm not insane now.* The last one read: *Give my love to Angie.*'

Astourde closed his notebook, and returned it to the drawer He looked back at Wentik.

'That is the entire information that I, or anybody else, had before you were brought to the Planalto District.'

Wentik stood up. It occurred to him that the relationship between Astourde and himself was now totally reversed. The process had begun the day before when he reacted violently against his interrogation, and was consummated in the expectant silence with which Astourde now waited, as if for Wentik's judgment.

He walked to the window, and looked out into the blackness of the night on the plain. So often in the past he had sat in this room and looked at the horizon, wondering where in hell he really was and whether what Musgrove had told him had been anywhere near a true representation. What he had been told that day, when he and Musgrove had walked out of the jungle and across some dividing line incomprehensible and irreversible, had been in essence no more or less than what Astourde had just told him. But now there was an important difference, he could think and act on his own initiative, and the information available to him contained more meaning.

But the plain lay beneath his gaze, dark and mysterious.

Astourde said: 'You are wondering how I became involved with this.'

'Partly,' Wentik said, no longer curious.

'I wish I could tell you all that happened between then and now. Unhappily,' and his voice reflected the tone of his thoughts, 'I was subjected to intense cross-examination about what had been seen, as were all the men. The photographs we took at the time, the sworn statements of all those that saw what happened when the aircraft landed nearby ... this is what changed things.

'Then I came across a report on your work and I took up the matter with the subcommittee. I was given a budget to work with, a time-limit in which to produce results and a free hand to take you off your work.'

Wentik stood with his back to the window, and looked at the litde man sitting at the desk. He represented the administrative might of government, yet his chain of responsibility led to an obscure subcommittee somewhere in Washington whose origins had been forgotten, and whose attentions were probably directed elsewhere. Yet this administrative system had given Astourde power of movement over Wentik.

And anyway, what the hell did his work have to do with this?

'It seems to me,' he said, 'that the crux of everything comes down to this. You keep referring to my work, as if that explained everything.'

'Well, doesn't it?'

'I don't see why.'

'You published a paper about the chemical reaction of the brain?'

'Yes.'

'And a proposal that the normal working of the brain could

be artificially displaced, either permanently or temporarily, with drugs?'

Wentik said: 'That was while I was still with the Genex Corporation, in Minneapolis. It was as a result of that paper that I got a government research-grant, and was moved to Antarctica.'

'And also,' Astourde added, 'that you're here now. It seemed to me that if what the man Brander had said were so, however incredible it may seem, then most of the physical mystery surrounding the region would be explained. Together with what we'd found from the stroboscopic tests it indicated to me that the Planalto District was an area of land somehow artificially displaced into the future. Or, what was more likely or probable, a piece of land from the future existing in the present.

'If this were the case, then that future would be every bit as real as our present and would be an outcome, however far removed, of what is happening now.'

Wentik said: 'Musgrove was saying something like this.'

'Yes. But the difference is that Musgrove himself knows nothing about the mental changes that take place on entering the District. This is my own surmise, and I have told no one about it except you. It was Brander, when he twice talked about insanity, that started my thinking. This puzzled me until I read about your work.

'Until this time I could no better explain what I had seen than anyone else. But your work was the link. I suddenly guessed that if several men became schizophrenic simultaneously, then there was probably some external explanation for it.'

'Such as a chemical or drug?' Wentik said.

'Yes. Precisely. Just as you were working on in Antarctica.'

Wentik walked back to the desk, and planted his hands firmly on the edge. He put his face close to Astourde's.

'Fine,' he said harshly. 'And you're here, and I'm here, and a dozen other men are here – and none of us can get back. Did you know this would happen?'

Astourde shook his head miserably.

'No, Elias.'

He got up, and walked to the door. He turned and looked at Wentik. Something about his expression reminded Wentik of the closing stages of the interrogation on the lawn. The sense of defeat hung like heavy layers of flesh on his bearing.

'Would you open the door, please?' he said.

Wentik took the key from his pocket, and complied. Astourde stepped through into the corridor.

'Wait here,' he said.' I'll get you the maps.'

He disappeared down the short corridor, and Wentik went back to the desk. He sat down, feeling again the full weight of the bleakness of his situation. He'd learned only one thing really new to him this evening: that Astourde and the others were subject to periods of intermittent insanity. He thought again of his first day in the District, when Musgrove had run berserk at the mill ... Now at least there was a partial explanation for that. In addition, the general behaviour of the other men could be explained in terms of irrational inconsequence.

He could understand Astourde better, as well. Potentially, he was now a classic case of the criminal mind, incipiently paranoiac, capable of any irrational act.

But why was he, Wentik himself, immune to what was going on?

His only thought was that the few times he'd taken minute quantities of the drugs himself, he'd been able to build up a personal resistance to them. But all this presupposed Astourde's theory: that in some manner the atmosphere of this future place was sown with drugs that he himself had developed.

What had happened? His work had been direcdy sponsored by the government for peaceful purposes, and as far as he knew it would have no military application. But was it possible that a corrupted, sophisticated version of his drug had been used as a weapon?

Wentik shook his head, and stood up again. He walked to the window.

Outside, someone had lighted several arc-lamps and a brilliant flood of light covered the ground at the front of the jail. In the glare, the dull-green helicopter could be plainly seen. A figure was inside it, moving about.

Abrupdy he came to the hatch, and dropped to the floor. It was

Astourde, and he was carrying what looked like a jerrican.

As Wentik watched, he ran towards the jail. After a moment or two, the lights went out.

What the hell was he doing? Wentik wondered.

He walked back to the desk, and leaned against its edge. A minute later, Astourde came into the office carrying the jerrican in his right hand.

In his left hand he held an automatic rifle.

He put down the jerrican, and transferred the rifle to his right hand. The safety-catch slid back with a distinct noise.

Astourde said: 'All right, Doctor Wentik. Pick up the can.'

'What are you doing, Astourde? Don't make yourself even more ridiculous.'

'I know what I'm doing. *Pick it up!*'

Wentik stepped towards him and Astourde backed away slightly. It was impossible to make a lunge for the rifle. Wentik stooped and picked up the jerrican. It was heavy, almost full of aviation-spirit.

'Now go downstairs.'

Astourde waved the muzzle of the weapon along the corridor, and Wentik walked through the door.

The two men walked slowly through the jail, the way they had come an hour earlier when returning from the shack. At Astourde's direction, Wentik headed down to the rear entrance of the jail. They met no one on the way.

At the light wooden door, he paused. Astourde prodded his back with the rifle.

'Get outside, Doctor Wentik!'

Astourde followed him through the door and on to the lawn. It was as dark as extinction, the sky covered with a uniform layer of low, dense cloud that admitted no light.

Wentik remembered the torch in his pocket, and wondered whether in the dark he could snatch it out and fell Astourde. Before he could even consider the thought a beam of light surrounded him. The man had equipped himself with one.

Astourde pointed with the beam of light.

'That way!'

The two men set off across the darkened plain.

Ten

•

They stopped at the shack, facing one of the four entrances to it. Astourde shone his torch on to it.

'Inside, Doctor Wentik. It will be warmer there.'

He tapped the barrel of his rifle meaningfully against the jerrican, and a surge of alarm rose in Wentik's mind. Could the man really intend to kill him?

The rifle jabbed sharply into his backbone and, reluctantly, Wentik moved forward. He pushed through the door, and into the first tunnel. He came to the door at the end, which was closed. Astourde had followed him inside.

'Go through,' he said, his voice muffled in the confined space.

Wentik pushed it, and it swung to the right, exposing the tunnel which branched off to the left. The rifle prodded him again.

'Go on.'

Wentik walked down the next tunnel, with Astourde close on his heels. The door at the end here was closed, and he stopped by it.

Astourde said: 'Keep going, Doctor Wentik. Let's get right into the centre of it, shall we?'

He pushed the door open with the neck of the rifle, and behind them Wentik heard the first door close with its quiet thump. Did Astourde know about the workings of the maze? he asked himself. Did he know that he was caught inside it just as much as himself?

At Astourde's direction, he pressed on. They passed down a dozen tunnels, branching irregularly to the left and right as dictated by the movement of the hatches. Then Astourde stopped him.

'Put down the can, Doctor Wentik.'

Gratefully, he let it down to the floor. For the last few minutes it had been weighing heavily on his arm.

Although the torch shone towards him, Wentik could vaguely make out the shape of Astourde next to him. He thought: You're trapping yourself again, Astourde.

Just as his realization the day before, that the Planalto District was as much a prison to Astourde as it was to himself, had enabled him to break free of the psychological grip in which he'd been held, so he saw now that Astourde could no more get out of the maze than he could. And furthermore, Astourde's orientation around objects – the rifle, the torch and the jerrican, of which he could handle only two at any one time – had led him to situation where he was incapable of movement without Wentik's help.

Wentik watched the man with distorted amusement. How was he going to sort this one out?

With the transparent simplicity of a child, Astourde said: 'Hold the torch, Doctor Wentik.'

The rifle was still trained on him. Wentik took the torch, and pointed it directly into the other man's eyes.

Then he switched it out.

In the sudden darkness he dived towards the next door and ran through. He hurled the torch towards where he guessed Astourde's head would be, but heard it smash against a wall. He turned and ran blindly, his hands pressed against each side wall for guidance. If he could reach the next door before Astourde could get through that one, then the man would be unable to follow him. He ran crouching down the tunnel, groping to make contact with the next door. Behind him the rifle suddenly roared, making a terrible racket in the claustrophobic closeness of the corridors, and light flashed around him.

He bounced painfully against a wall as he rounded the bend. There was no door to open! He'd reached an open stretch.

He ran on with Astourde behind him, less hampered by the low ceilings because of his smaller stature.

The next door was also open, and the tunnel angled to the right. Again he fled blindly down the tunnel. The rifle fired again.

How many shots has he got? thought Wentik.

As he ran he felt in the pockets of the white coat. He managed to switch on the torch just as he came to the next door. This one was closed. He pushed through it, and ran on. Astourde was still behind him.

The next door was closed, and he pushed against that. Suddenly, Astourde was no longer with him, and all was quiet.

He went back to the door that he had closed by opening the other one, and listened at it. Behind, he could hear Astourde moving. The man was confused.

As Wentik knew from his experiments in the maze that afternoon, there was no way of opening a door from that side. Where Astourde was standing was inside the triangle described by the door's movements. The door could only be moved from the outside of the triangle; that is, from pushing against it from the tunnel it blocked off.

Now he had to be careful. If Astourde were to move in either direction open to him, and push against the next door he found, then this one would open. Did he know that?

Wentik thought: The next man to open a door will change all the others. If Astourde does it and comes back here, he'll catch me. On the other hand, if I do it we'll be separated by mathematical probabilities he knows nothing about …

His mind made up, he ran back down the corridor, past the door he had opened, and came to the next one. Now … He pushed it, and went through. He flashed his torch down the corridor, the next one was open. He moved towards it.

Just before he got there, it closed.

Astourde! The man was now moving through the maze as he was. No longer did Wentik alone control the movement of the doors.

He flashed the light over the door, then listened at it. He could hear nothing. Astourde did not seem to be anywhere near. He was just about to push against the door, when it opened of its own accord.

Astourde had moved again.

Where the hell was he?

Paradoxically, Astourde now had a kind of advantage. It appeared that he had no idea of the implications of opening a door, and thus was innocent of the fact that every time he moved he changed the whole layout of the maze. At any moment, thought Wentik, he would come around the corner ... And from any direction. Further, Wentik had the only torch and although he could use it to see where he was going, and in a confrontation would have the advantage, as long as he didn't know where Astourde was there was more chance of him seeing the glow from the torch before Wentik could actually see him. Wentik switched it off.

Now he felt the odds were level. As blind as Astourde in the impenetrable blackness, he had as good a chance of getting out of the maze as Astourde had of catching him.

The door before him moved again, closing the tunnel to the left and exposing the one to the right.

Cautiously, Wentik felt his way down it. Let Astourde move the doors. That way at least he wouldn't open a door to find Astourde behind it. At the end of this tunnel the door was open, exposing the left tunnel, closing the right one. Wentik waited for a moment, and he heard it close.

He could hear no sound of Astourde, though the man must be somewhere near.

The door closed off his tunnel. He waited motionlessly.

Then it moved again, and the right tunnel was exposed, the left one closed. He moved on warily.

In the dark he stumbled. The jerrican!

His route through the maze had brought him back to where he had started. Petrol poured from the open nozzle in the top, spilling across the floor.

Footsteps approached.

Wentik leaped to his feet, and banged his head painfully against the top of the tunnel. Astourde was close! He stood perfectly still, uncertain in which direction he should move.

The door to his left opened. Wentik stepped sideways towards it. Only a few feet ...

At the end, the door blocked his way. Astourde had come through the one at the other end, and this one had closed!

Astourde said, his voice high and shrill: 'You're here, aren't you, Elias?'

Not waiting for an answer he fired the rifle, blindly and without aim. The bullet thudded into the door over Wentik's head.

Blinded by the flash he shouted: 'Stop shooting, Astourde! There's petrol here!'

He stepped backwards quickly, pushing through the door. Behind him, he heard Astourde scramble after him. He ran quickly down the tunnel, in his haste accidentally dropping his torch. Not pausing, he pushed through the next door, then the next one. If Astourde were still by the jerrican, his way would be blocked. Wentik leaned against the tunnel wall, fighting for breath.

Again he was in uncertain darkness. He could hear nothing. What was Astourde going to do with the petrol?

Then, not far away, he heard the muffled roar of the rifle. Astourde was shooting blindly. Another shot fired. Then again.

Wentik moved to the next door, and leaned his weight against it tiredly. It gave, and he stumbled through. He walked to the next door, and pushed against that, but it wouldn't move. He pushed again, but it still didn't give. Was Astourde blocking it in some way?

Then he realized: it was the last door!

He pulled it gratefully, and came out on to the stubble. The only doors in the maze that were opened by pulling led into the open.

Outside, he stopped. Where was Astourde now?

He stepped to the side of the shack, and put his ear against the wooden wall. Somewhere inside the rifle fired again, its noise only partially deadened by the thin wood.

Wentik put his mouth up to the wall, and cupped his hands round.

'Astourde! Stop firing that rifle! The place is full of petrol.' In reply, he heard Astourde shout: 'I'll find you, Wentik! I know you're here!'

Another shot, and Astourde screamed.

A sudden blaze of light appeared along the base of the wall, and Wentik leaped backwards. Flames gushed from the door he had just come through. There was a loud concussion, and part of the wall fell away, revealing a solid mass of white fire.

Astourde screamed again.

Wentik backed farther away, caught his heel on some projection and fell on to the stubble. He rolled on to his side and crawled from the blaze.

Inside the ramshackle building, Astourde screamed again and again, then stopped abruptly. There was nothing, absolutely nothing, Wentik could do. He stood up about twenty yards away and stood facing the conflagration, radiant heat threatening to blister his face.

As other parts of the maze started to catch, and the wooden partitions inside curled and shredded in the heat, Wentik turned his back and started to walk slowly towards the jail.

Fifty yards away, in a silent semi-circle, the rest of the men stood, their white coats reflecting the orange inferno in the night.

Eleven

•

The following evening, Wentik sat alone in Astourde's old office and studied the makeshift maps that the man had brought with him.

There were only four, and the information he had been able to glean from them was minimal.

The first one, potentially of the greatest value, had been the biggest disappointment. It was a large-scale map of part of the Brazilian Mato Grosso and, judging from the ballpoint circles that someone had made on the small-scale map of the whole of Brazil on the outside, it was approximately the part of the jungle in which the jail was situated.

The scale was comprehensive, one inch to the mile, yet the information it gave was virtually nonexistent. It was the kind of map no one other than specialist geographers or geologists ever sees. Obviously drawn from satellite photography, the map was covered with various symbols indicating types of jungle growth, humidity and temperature at different times of the year, contour-lines (widely spaced and meandering), and several streams and small rivers. Beyond this, nothing at all.

If the whole of the Mato Grosso were covered by maps of this scale, as indeed it appeared (the map was numbered), then there were evidently many thousands of them stored away in a dusty reference-room in some government building.

Wentik wondered for a moment at the patience and single-mindedness of the cartographers who had worked on the series.

The second map was a political map of the whole of the South

American continent, showing current lines of nationality and all major cities. He looked closely at the tiny print and was able to pick out Porto Velho, and for the first time appreciated the staggering size of the continent, and how far into the centre of it he now was.

Astourde's third map was more of a plan. It showed in great detail the layout of the whole of the Concentration in Antarctica. Wentik, knowing the immense secrecy with which the Concentration had been built, and the detailed security-screening that went on before anyone was transferred there, was amazed again at the apparent ease with which Astourde had had access to documents like this and the facilities to take him from his work.

The last so-called map was another plan, this time drawn roughly in pencil. It showed a great circle with the jail as its central point. In the bottom right-hand corner of the sheet was initialled *C.V.A.* What had the *V* stood for? Wentik wondered.

If Astourde had drawn this, Wentik thought, he didn't know much about cartography. According to the rough scale along the bottom, the diameter of the field was about six miles. If this were so, then he had drawn the jail hopelessly out of scale. And his sense of direction was all wrong. The front of the jail, where his office was situated, faced to the south. The sun came almost direcdy overhead at noon, but to the north. And for some reason Astourde had drawn the jail as being a long rectangle, whereas it was more nearly a square. The mast, which Wentik knew was to the north-west of the jail, was drawn on the plan as a dot to the top right-hand corner of the jail.

Wentik also noticed, with some curiosity, that Astourde had not drawn in the windmill, which stood some two or three miles away in the direction from which he and Musgrove had come, the south-west.

He tried to figure out where it should be on Astourde's plan, but gave up the attempt quickly. It was too confusing. Partly because of Astourde's inaccurate drawing, and also because Wentik had been uncertain of the southern hemisphere north/south inversion ever since he'd been in Brazil.

It had been different in Antarctica. There were only two directions there: north and south.

The thought of the windmill made him realize for the first time that when he and Musgrove had arrived at the jail they had come from the south-west. And yet Porto Velho lay clearly to the north-west. The route that Musgrove had brought them had not, Wentik mused, been the most direct.

In his mind's eye he tried to superimpose Astourde's plan on to the featureless one-inch map of the area. Thinking of the vast plain of stubble, it was hard to reconcile it with the knowledge that if he could somehow return to what was his present he would be in dense jungle.

He recalled what had happened when he had walked into the District with Musgrove. They had gone several paces before Wentik had noticed that the jungle behind them had vanished. It hadn't in reality, of course, but had disappeared into what then had become the past. Or was it he who had vanished into the future? What would have happened, Wentik wondered curiously, if he had looked round at the instant he crossed over? One leg in the past (or present) and one leg in the future (or present). Standing on the edge of the District and looking in, one could see quite clearly into it. Yet it didn't work the other way.

What would happen if someone inside, being observed by another person *outside,* were to walk directly towards the dividing line? Would he vanish, or would he return to the present?

Or what?

Wentik closed the maps, and put them inside a drawer in the desk. At any rate, they suggested no way out of this situation.

As ever, his main preoccupation was to get back to what he knew as a normal life. He wanted to see his wife and children. He wanted to get back to his work, particularly now that the end was almost in sight. And Astourde's death would have to be reported. There would be an inquiry no doubt. And Musgrove too; the man had disappeared and, as far as Wentik knew, was no longer anywhere near the jail.

His immediate plan was basic: return to Porto Velho.

Taking into consideration his isolation in the Mato Grosso, getting across to the coast was out of the question. Porto Velho was nothing spectacular in the way of cities, but it did have telephones and radio, and was situated on the Madeira river. The airstrip there was not much more than a piece of cleared land, but at least it had the facilities for flight.

This was the Porto Velho he had seen and it was difficult, without evidence to the contrary, to conceive of it in any other way. If he was to accept what Musgrove and Astourde had told him, that the jail existed in a state of future time, then if he flew to Porto Velho he didn't know for certain what he would find.

He felt instinctively that it would be just as he'd left it; that to leave the District would be as simple as entering it.

So in the morning he intended to fly there.

He had found one of the men, a short, fair-skinned man named Robbins, who was the helicopter's pilot, and the machine had been made airworthy once more. He and Robbins were going to leave the next day. If they got to Porto Velho safely, Robbins would return to the jail and pick up the other men, while Wentik started out for civilization.

It was a crude plan, but it was all he could manage.

He stood up, and walked out into the corridor.

There was just one more thing about this place he wanted to resolve before the morning: the object he had seen the day before from the top of the mast. A light-coloured protuberance from the wall of the jail, placed with apparent randomness and lack of purpose. There had been something vaguely familiar about its shape that he had not been able to define …

The jail was quiet, and although the cells being used by the other men were in this part of the building, Wentik could hear no noise. Perhaps they were asleep. He came to the main staircase, walked quickly down it and came out into the open air.

It was cold, and there was a chill wind blowing across the plain.

Wentik shivered, and tightened the white coat across his chest. The sky was clear, and the stars shone down brightly. He started to walk along the perimeter of the building, towards the southwest corner.

Astourde's continued insistence on Wentik's work still intrigued him. It was hard to see how it had anything to do with his present situation, but that could be explained by either a lack of Astourde's understanding of what he had been doing, or a development of his work of which he had no knowledge.

He wondered at the man's process of thought to connect the two. It was possible that he had had some scientific training. Only some, not much. His interest in Wentik's earlier work was unusual, if only because what he had been doing was of esoteric academic interest. Astourde must then have been in some position where he could have normal access to the papers that had been published. Otherwise, how could he have come across them?

During the early days of his work with the Genex Corporation, he'd been conducting an investigation into what could loosely be called the chemistry of sanity. If this was an imprecise description, then it was apt, for Wentik's field was not really connected with research into the workings of the human brain. He'd been more interested in the external factors of insanity, how ideas or images could distort rational thought. How even incidental factors such as environment or diet could ultimately affect sanity. His work at this time had been largely exploratory, with no known purpose in view. He needed to spend a lot of money in his work, and have virtually unlimited resources for experiment. The English university to which he'd been attached had been unable to provide these, and with a feeling of transient regret, Wentik had flown to Minneapolis for a six-months trial period.

If all went well, his family would have followed him over at the end of that time.

The few papers that Genex had allowed him to publish must have been the ones that came into Astourde's hands. But if the man had worked in any field even faintly parallel to Wentik's he would have had sufficient scientific acumen to realize that what was called insanity in general terms was not a scientific description.

Insanity is a legal definition, not a medical one.

During that cryptic conversation with Johns, the man had said that Astourde 'blamed' Wentik for what was happening here. That could be translated to mean that although Astourde had brought him here with official backing, it was for some obscure purpose of his own; perhaps to inflict some kind of punishment. Would that explain the interrogation?

The most puzzling factor was that even if it were granted that Astourde had correctly read and understood Wentik's work, and that his work did have a rational connection with the Planalto District, then it must have been a considerable piece of deductive thought to connect the two.

Wentik shook his head. He just didn't believe Astourde was capable of it. However much he might have known about Wentik's research for Genex, he could have had no conception of what he was doing at the Concentration.

Four months after Wentik had started work in Minneapolis, he'd been approached by representatives of a government research department, and had been offered the job in Antarctica. Genex had agreed to release him for the necessary time, and the government were willing to provide him with all the resources he required. Wentik aimed high; asked for and got a full laboratory, a team of highly trained assistants, and complete independence, and found himself a few weeks later six hundred feet beneath the Antarctic ice-cap.

The major disadvantage to this, from Wentik's point of view, was the prolonged separation from his family. But his wife had taken it philosophically; already resigned to six months of separation, she had felt that a few more would not matter in the long run.

At the Concentration his work had taken a new tack. Instead of merely experimenting with possible affectives to sanity, Wentik began to try to discover positive agents.

Working at first with scopolamine-derivatives, Wentik had tried to find a chemical parallel to Pavlov's work. Pavlov had devoted his life to the science of indoctrination, working on dogs so that after a prolonged series of stimuli they would behave in certain predetermined ways. Pavlov's conditioning medium had been emotional experience, using flashing lights, electric shock, starvation and other kinds of intimidation. His methods worked with the passage of time, but Wentik wanted to short-cut the process chemically. What three months of reflexive training could teach a dog or a rat Wentik had cut to three days, in laboratory conditions, by the use of intracortical injection. Within weeks of getting down to the work, Wentik had been able in two days to change the rats in his laboratory from ferocious, carnivorous vermin to docile lap-pets.

Two other rats, conditioned by Pavlovian methods, had made no measurable progress since the start of the experiment.

But as far as Wentik was concerned, his work was still in its earliest stages. For a start, the compound was administered by injection and he and N'Goko had wanted to be able to produce the effects with solids or gases. And the second complication, by far the more serious, was that if the drug were administered with anything like the strength needed to do what it should, then the subject invariably died soon after.

Although Wentik had injected himself with the drug, he knew that the quantities he had taken were far from toxic; but equally, that they were insufficiently strong to have affected him in the way intended.

In effect it was a method of increasing human intelligence, though administered incorrectly it could be extremely dangerous. A man taking the compound in its correct strength would lose his identity, become amnesiac, would perhaps revert to a savage or bestial state. On the other hand, the same man subjected to the right stimuli could be conditioned to an entirely new identity.

It was a development with devastating potential and one which would, if Wentik had been allowed to finish his work, have perhaps completely altered existing methods of crime-detection, political indoctrination or religious teaching.

But there was no way Astourde could have known this. From the time Wentik had been at the Concentration, he'd had no contact with the outside world beyond a weekly letter to his wife, and in that he rarely mentioned his work. Only N'Goko and his other assistants knew what the work involved, but they were as isolated at the Concentration as he was.

Astourde had implied that the atmosphere here was sown in some way with a drug or gas which induced insanity, yet how could he have connected this with Wentik? It didn't tie in. The causes and effects were becoming confused. Wentik was brought here by Astourde because he was to blame for the atmospheric environment, yet Astourde had no sure way of knowing about it until he got here.

Wentik had reached the corner of the building, and he paused for a moment.

Somehow, he felt, there was a huge mistake behind all this. Astourde had paid for it, if that was so, but the man's death could not be the end of it.

He moved on along the western side of the jail, walking more slowly and scanning the wall above him. Along this side there were fewer apertures in the wall than in other places. It was quiet here and dark, sheltered from the wind. The moon, which was in its last phase, was on the other side of the jail and the whole, face of the wall was in sombre shadow.

He reached the next corner of the jail without seeing anything and started back again, his earlier curiosity re-aroused. It had been about halfway along this wall.

Wentik stopped as a slight protuberance from the sheer wall suddenly registered itself dimly. It was easy to miss in the dark. He flattened himself against the base of the wall and looked up so that the object was silhouetted against the starry sky.

There was something familiar about it . . .

He fumbled in the pockets of his coat for his torch, pulled it out and switched it on. Stepping back from the wall, he directed the beam upwards.

The object, its presence only too obvious, its purpose only too obscure, sat squarely in the beam of light.

An ear.

A huge human ear growing from the wall, like the hand had grown from the table.

Wentik switched off his torch abruptly, and stepped back another two paces, his heart unaccountably beating faster.

Twelve

•

There is an element of terror in any natural object that does not exist in its proper place. Wentik experienced the full force of this as he stood in the dark.

A hand grows from a table, and an ear from a wall. A maze is constructed to a sophisticated mathematical formula, yet is housed in a tumbledown shack. A minor official terrorizes me, and a man tries to fly a helicopter without vanes. Land exists in future time, though I feel and believe instinctively that I am in the present. Irrational behaviour creates a reaction-pattern of its own.

What else will this place do to me?

For a few seconds the ear on the wall was invisible, then, as his eyes became reaccustomed to the dark, it hung before him, tantalizingly near but not within reach. Perhaps it was twelve feet from the ground, its own height being about four feet.

He switched on his torch again, and experienced a minor version of his first shock of realization.

Wentik shone his torch over the part of the wall immediately next to the ear. There were very few windows along this side, and it would be difficult to re-locate it precisely from the inside of the jail. He estimated that it would be on the second storey of the building, perhaps one hundred yards from the north-western corner.

The same curiosity that he had experienced with the hand, coming as a natural outcome of his first shock, drove him to find out what he could about it. There was an unbelievable illogicality to some of the features of this jail, even though the four-square building, alone on a barren plain and surrounded by hundreds of square miles of the close-shorn stubble made it an eminently suitable site for a prison.

If, Wentik added to himself as an afterthought, that was the original purpose of the building.

With one last look at the ear in the light from the torch, Wentik walked towards the south face of the jail again, and the main entrance. He was now feeling decidedly cold, and he moved quickly.

Inside the building again, he walked up the main flight of stairs and rounded the corner off the first-floor landing. There was a short corridor here, and he walked down it to the end. A metal door constructed of heavy bars blocked the way, but he pushed it aside.

Before him now lay the long corridor on the second storey of the western wing.

As he looked along it, the line of cell-doors was on his left. On the floors above and below this one, Wentik knew that the cells were on the right of the corridor. It made for a uniform asymmetricality of design that had confused Wentik in his first days wandering along the corridors.

From where he had emerged out of the side corridor he was nearest to the southern end of the jail, so he walked down the long passage. At intervals he stopped and peered into some of the cells he was passing. Most of them were built to the same design. This was not the side of the jail Astourde and his men had chosen for their quarters, and everything was virtually untouched. The door to each cell was metal, fitted with judas window and shutter operable from the outside only. There were two bolts, top and bottom, and a heavy mortice lock. The hinges, crude and ill-designed plates of metal, were on the outside of the door.

Inside the cells there was usually one bunk or two, never more. Few cells had access to daylight, and in those that had, the windows were tiny panes of frosted glass protected with one or two iron bars. There was little apparent planning in the design of the cells. The only object seemed to be a minimum of space and a maximum of discomfort.

When Wentik was what he estimated to be a hundred yards from the far end of the corridor, he stopped. Somewhere around here on the outside wall was the ear. He stepped back a few yards and opened the door of the nearest cell. It was no different from any of the others.

He moved slowly along the corridor, aware that the doors of the cells were farther apart than the space occupied warranted. What was between the cells?

The sixth door he tried he found was wedged tight. Not locked, but held in place as if either the frame or the door itself had warped. He put his shoulder to it, and pushed hard.

The door grated open.

Inside, it was dark. To the right of the door, on the wall, he found a light-switch. The room exploded into brilliant light, far brighter than the illumination in any other part of the jail.

He walked in, and looked around the cell.

With two exceptions, it was like every other one had had seen at the jail. The walls were of drab-painted metal, the concrete floor was bare, and the only furnishing was the hard bunk against one of the walls.

What made it exceptional was the size – it was at least twice the width of a normal cell – and the presence of the machine taking up most of the space against the far wall.

It occupied the whole height of the wall, reaching to within a couple of inches of the ceiling. In the harsh light of the bulb it gleamed dully, its metal sides scoured to a matt intensity. The side facing Wentik was almost totally devoid of feature; just a black wall of metal.

He went across to it, and put his hand against it.

To his surprise it was warm, and vibrated almost imperceptibly beneath his fingertips.

He walked to the side of the machine and found there was just enough room for a man of average build to squeeze between it and the wall. As at the front of the machine, the side carried no noticeable external markings.

Just as he had recoiled at the appearance of the ear on the wall, Wentik found he was again shrinking from the acceptance of this. By its sheer feeling of functionality, it became anomalous. So accustomed was he becoming to irrational and apparently purposeless features that his mind baulked at something which only a few weeks earlier would have been a normal part of his working life.

A computer? Here?

His mind leaped at the explanation even while a part of it refused to accept it.

Wentik moved back to the door of the cell, leaned against it and regarded the machine.

In the brightly lit room it was a negative factor. An understatement of mechanical design contrasting with the extrovert bleakness of the rest of the jail. A smoothly machined construction of metal, out of place in the dilapidated surroundings of the abandoned jail. Featureless, and silent. Hidden from view only by random placement. Solid and symmetrical, and purposeful in an environment of doubt and irrationalism.

Wentik wondered whether Astourde had known of its existence.

He walked across to it again, recalling that he had only discovered himself by chance. His clue, the ear on the wall, he had forgotten momentarily in the surprise of finding this.

He squeezed his body down the right-hand side of the computer, between it and the wall of the cell.

When he reached the far wall, the one direcdy against the outside of the jail, Wentik paused. In the confined space it was difficult to turn his head. He moved back slightly, eased his shoulders at an angle towards the wall, and craned his neck.

Between the casing of the computer and the wall, there was a space of about four feet. Wentik wriggled round the corner, and stood in the space. Here it was slightly darker than in the rest of the cell, receiving no direct light from the bulb in the centre of the ceiling.

On this side of the computer was a long array of dials and meters. Wentik peered at them with interest, but saw none that he could recognize. Beside them was a row of toggle switches, all in the down position, and at the end of these a groove like a three-pointed star was cut into the wall of the machine with a lever switch resting in the neutral position.

At the top of the machine, at about the same level as his forehead, there was an induction grille. Somewhere behind it ran a silent fan, for he could feel a gentle flow of air into it as he passed his hand in front.

But the most obvious feature here was an arrangement of levers, one coming out of the side of the computer and the other from the wall, meeting at an apex in the space between like two hands clasped in a trial of strength. The point at which they met was several feet from the ground, each lever being approximately two and a half feet long and coming out of the wall and computer at an angle of about sixty degrees from the perpendicular. Wentik could walk beneath the point of contact without stooping.

Did the outer lever connect in some way with the huge ear on the outside wall?

He reached up and touched the ball-joint where the two levers met. They were locked immovably, yet a dial on the side of the machine unaccountably jumped. He touched the inner lever near the point where it disappeared into the body of the machine, and several more dials moved suddenly.

He selected one of the toggle switches at random, and flicked it upwards. Nothing, apparently, happened. No dials moved, no sound could be heard. He selected another, and there was still no response.

Was the machine operational? If so, did the switches have any function? He bent down, but could see no inscriptions anywhere near the switches that might give some idea as to their function.

His attention shifted to the switch inside the three-way groove.

As his fingers touched it, he found that it moved easily. He pressed it directly upwards, and saw that next to it a tiny panel lit up. He looked closely and saw the letters 'AA' alight. He pulled the switch down again, and they flicked off. He moved it down and to the right, and in another panel the letter 'A' came alight. Back to the centre, and it flicked off.

As he moved it downwards and to the left, two separate things happened. A panel lit up with the letters 'BB' on it, and something inside the cabinet of the machine and on the other side of the arch of levers made a high-pitched whistling noise. After about five seconds it stopped. The panel continued to glow.

Wentik pushed the switch back to its central point, and the letters disappeared.

He walked under the two levers, and looked closely at the machine at the point from which the noise had come.

Almost at the top edge he saw a thin metal inspection plate, held on to the cabinet of the computer with a plain-headed rivet. He swung it aside, and found a small compartment. Inside was a long strip of cable.

Pulling it out carefully, he saw that the end of it had been separated into two finely pointed strands. He looked at it closely, but could see nothing that could have caused the noise.

He let the cable dangle down the side of the machine, and went back to the switch. He pressed it down to the left, the panel lit up, and again the whistling noise was emitted, this time much louder. He put his ear close to the ends of the cable, and found that it appeared to emanate from a point somewhere between the two strands. He was going to touch it, when the noise stopped abruptly.

He reached over to move the switch again, but something warned him to be careful. He looked at the cable again, then returned it gingerly to its compartment.

There was one more metal plate next to the cover and he looked at it, straining his eyes in the dim light. On it was engraved:

Companhia Nacional, Volta Redonda
Direct Power Corp SA 2184
Int Pat 41.463960412 TM Reg'd
S/N GH 4789 Mod 2001

After a few more minutes, in which he re-examined the various dials and switches, Wentik squeezed his way back past the side of the machine and came out into the main part of the cell. He looked at the machine standing there silently. Its aura of restrained power and unleashed energy was tremendous.

He moved to the door, put his hand on the light-switch, and looked around the cell once more.

And saw it for the first time.

In the centre of the floor, ground neglectfully by a heel against the concrete, was the stub of a black-papered cigarette.

Thirteen

•

The following morning Wentik took off in the helicopter for Porto Velho. With him and the pilot went Johns. The three men sat cramped up against each other in the perspex-surrounded cockpit, and as the sun was shining full on to them they had all removed their coats and sat in their shirts only. The pilot, Robbins, had taken the machine up to about two thousand feet, circled the jail, and then at Wentik's instruction had flown in a north-westerly direction towards Porto Velho.

The plain below presented the same drab aspect from the air as it did from the ground; dead, lacklife stubble.

He shouted to Robbins over the racket of the engine: 'How far have we gone?'

The man shrugged.

Johns said: 'About three miles, sir.'

Wentik nodded, and looked in the direction in which they were flying. From this height the range of visibility would probably be several miles, except that today there was a good deal of heat-haze.

A new thought struck Wentik, and he wondered why it hadn't occurred to him before. Assume that a large area of the jungle *had* been cleared. Would this have a long-term climatic effect? From what he remembered, this part of Brazil was one of the wettest areas of the world. Yet the rain at the jail was spasmodic, coming down either during the night or in the early mornings. (Before take-off this morning, they had had to wait for an hour for the rain to stop before they could leave.) Mostly during the day the sky was clear and blue, the sun hot. Would the absence of jungle-growth make any difference to the formation of clouds, and hence to rainfall?

Secondary to this, the sheer physical task of clearing an area of jungle this size was beyond his conception.

And the farther they flew, with the plain below giving no sign of reverting to its natural self, the more it seemed that their destination would not be the one Wentik hoped to find.

Johns touched his arm, and pointed down through the perspex. Coming dimly into view through the haze were four black cubical constructions. Wentik craned his neck but could make out no feature on them that could tell him what they were.

'What are they?' he shouted.

'No idea,' Johns replied.

The pilot flew on. Wentik looked down eagerly.

'Do you want me to land, sir?' the pilot asked.

'No. Keep on going. Bring her down about five hundred feet, though.'

The pilot complied, and Wentik watched the objects as they slipped by underneath. From this elevation it was difficult to assess their size correctly, but he estimated that they were between twenty and thirty feet wide, and about fifty feet long. Were they in some way connected with the creation of the Planalto District?

They flew on steadily, the temperature in the cockpit mounting slowly. It was becoming really unpleasant now, even with all the vents and ports open. The heat of the engine, mounted in the compartment behind Wentik's seat, did nothing to make conditions in the cockpit any easier.

Quite suddenly, there was a marked change in the surface of the ground. Bushes appeared beneath them, and the savannah grass that was shorn to stubble everywhere else, grew wildly and unchecked. Trees appeared at intervals, and the undergrowth became dense and tangled.

They flew on for ten more minutes as the trees gradually thickened into full jungle. Wentik looked at it with a feeling of indefinable gratitude. Hostile as it was, the jungle represented to him a contact with normality of which he was in great need.

He said to Johns: 'How far are we from the jail now?'

'About twenty miles, sir.'

'And what's the total distance to Porto Velho?'

Johns looked at the map which Wentik had given him.

'Just over four hundred miles,' he said.

'What's the range of the helicopter?'

'We'll get there,' the pilot said.

Wentik nodded. He looked down at the jungle again. Brazilian rain-forest would probably look the same at any point in time. So ... were they now in what they knew as the present? Or were they still in the time of the Planalto District? There was no way of telling.

He said to the pilot: 'Climb.'

Robbins looked at him with a startled expression. Johns looked at him too. 'Climb, sir?'

'That's right. As high as this thing will go. We've got enough fuel.'

Obediendy, the pilot pulled on his control bar, and the pitch of the compressor increased. The machine started to climb effortlessly, ascending in a nose-up power stall that Wentik suddenly found exhilarating. He sat back in his seat, and watched the ground. The detail of vegetation began to dim with the haze, and formed a uniform carpet of dark green.

As the machine climbed, Wentik was reminded of an incident from his youth, when he'd spent a fortnight's holiday gliding in the weald of Kent. He'd gone up with an experienced pilot in an advanced competition soarer, to see for himself the difference between this and the powered flight to which he was more accustomed. They'd flown for the whole afternoon above the villages, fields and roads of the countryside. At one point they'd encountered a thermal above a freshly ploughed field simmering in the sunshine, and had climbed effortlessly and silendy in an ever-broadening spiral to ten thousand feet. The peace of that first long flight, and its feeling of freedom from the noise of life in London, had stayed with Wentik in memory for years after, and now he thought of it again as he climbed in an uncomfortable and noisy machine, above an alien and forbidding landscape.

Johns said to him, breaking his reverie: 'What do you want to do this for?'

Wentik looked at him. And said nothing.

He really had no idea of the reason behind his order. If anything, it was a subconscious feeling that if he could climb high enough, and far enough and perhaps fast enough, he could somehow scale the invisible barrier thrown up by the field surrounding the jail. This barrier kept him away from his family and his work, from civilization and, perhaps most subtly missed of all, his own time. For he was feeling now, more than ever before, a growing conviction that what his intellect had been trying to rationalize for weeks, and which now his whole body felt, was a fact.

He *was* somewhere in the future.

And this was the only way he could see a way back. If a rational approach should fail, act irrationally. Climb to the sky and achieve little. But stay on the ground and achieve nothing.

The pilot shouted: 'We're crossing ten thousand feet, sir!'

Wentik said: 'That'll do.'

It was a good height to fly at.

Once again the aircraft flew a straight course. Wentik looked keenly through the perspex port.

At his side, Johns seemed bored and distracted. The pilot was alert, his hands resting lightly on the controls.

Wentik was watching the surface of the ground. They had been in the air for nearly half an hour, and in that time he had seen no sign of human habitation. From this height no detail could be made out in the jungle, yet he kept his gaze directed downwards in the hope of finding a settlement at which they could land.

There was a sudden roar, and the helicopter rocked in its flight.

The pilot's hands tightened on the controls, and the euphoric drone of the engine broke into a snarl of power, then slackened immediately. The machine steadied.

Wentik looked round the sky. What had happened?

The roar came again, this time from below.

A jet aircraft was scudding away beneath them, banking sharply to the right and accelerating hard. Wentik saw the bright stab of after-burners in its jet exhausts. But it had moved too quickly for identification. Already it was out of sight.

'Did you recognize it?' he shouted to Johns, who was now sitting forward with his face alert.

'No. It was too quick.'

The jet came in from directly ahead, and flew a collision course straight at them. Robbins held the helicopter steady, and the jet dropped away beneath them at the last moment.

'The bastard!' Johns swore. 'What is it?'

Wentik said: 'I think it's a jet like the one Astourde photographed.'

The plane had banked again, and was now flying towards them from the port side. There was a brilliant flash, and something exploded immediately in front of the helicopter. The blast shook them, and they were through the hot black cloud of smoke before they had a chance to evade it.

The centuries-old shot across the bows. Unambiguous in meaning . . . Stop.

Wentik said to the pilot: 'I think he wants us to hover.'

'All right.'

The pilot lifted the nose of the craft, and adjusted the speed of the engine until their forward movement had stopped. 'Now what?' Johns muttered. 'Wait and see.'

Wentik looked around in an attempt to catch sight of the jet, but it had darted away again and he could see it nowhere. The pilot held the helicopter steady.

Johns said: 'There he is! Dead ahead.'

Wentik suddenly saw the jet as a speck of golden light. It was on another collision course.

He said to Robbins: 'Keep her steady.'

The plane seemed to be moving more slowly than it had before. About a hundred yards in front of the helicopter its nose lifted, and there was a spray of exhaust gases from a bank of VTOL jets mounted in its belly. In a curious skidding, stalling movement it stopped in front of the helicopter, and hovered no more than twenty feet from the cockpit.

Looking across at the pilot, Wentik realized that the man was sweating. Johns had shut his eyes.

'What do I do now, sir?' Robbins said.

'Be prepared to move fast,' Wentik said. 'But just hold this for the moment.'

The VTOL plane was moving slowly from side to side in front of them, the noise from its jets making the perspex canopy rattle and shake. As Wentik had seen in the photograph Astourde had shown him, there was no cockpit as such, apart from glass panels set flush into the sides of the front of the fuselage. Behind each of these he could dimly discern the figure of a man.

Almost imperceptibly, the jet was getting closer and its waving motion was becoming more pronounced. Wentik frowned. It was as if the men inside were trying to convey some message.

He looked closely at the VTOL as it crept towards them. It was painted a brilliant white, with its anhedral delta wings polished to a high metallic finish. The whole aircraft was huge, probably forty or fifty feet long. Its wings were short and stubby, with a span of no more than ten feet on each side, though they ran three-quarters of the length of the fuselage. There seemed to be no moving surfaces on the wings, but apart from this the overall shape of it was conventional.

One of the men inside the VTOL lifted a microphone or some gadget of similar purpose, and spoke into it. So close now were the two aircraft to each other that Wentik could quite clearly see the man's lips moving.

He looked for some markings on the side of the craft, but there was nothing that seemed to have any particular relevance. Beneath the forward edge of one of the wings was a block of lettering, but such was the angle that it was impossible to decipher them. On the underside of the other wing the letters TZN had been stencilled in bold, black lettering, and several panels along the forward part of the fuselage had what looked like instructions painted alongside them, but again he was unable to make out what they said.

The machine carried no apparent armament, though wing-tanks like fat white slugs were suspended near the fuselage.

The nose of the VTOL was less than ten feet away from them, when it dropped back quickly. When it was about thirty feet away, it came forward again, waggling its nose at them as before. Then it dropped back, and repeated it.

Suddenly, Wentik realized what it was they were trying to get across.

'I think they want us to go back,' he shouted to Robbins over the twin rackets of the engines.

'What? Back to the jail?' Johns said.

'I'm afraid so.'

'But if we do, we won't have enough fuel to get to Porto Velho another time.'

'I don't think the decision rests with us any longer.'

Robbins swung the control-bar, and the helicopter dropped down and to the right. He put it into a wide 180-degree turn, while the VTOL maintained its station above and behind them.

As the helicopter began its long, tumbling descent towards the plain and the jail, the aircraft followed them down at a discreet distance.

Robbins landed the helicopter outside the main entrance to the jail. It was noon.

Within three minutes, the VTOL jet landed twenty yards away, while Wentik and the other two sat down on the stubble in the shade of the helicopter.

Two men, wearing cumbersome gas-cylinders and face-masks, walked over to them laboriously. They stopped and looked down at the three men.

The taller of the two lifted off his face-mask.

'That's the one,' he said, pointing at Wentik.

The other man walked over quickly, holding a kind of metal tube. Before he could make any move to resist, Wentik saw a spurt of yellow vapour shoot out from the man's hand. The gas was bitter, and he inhaled some before he had time to hold his breath. A surge of warmth grew from the back of his head and worked round and into his face and eyes. As his consciousness faded rapidly, Wentik found himself looking irresistibly into the grinning, sardonic face of the man who had removed his mask.

It was Musgrove.

PART TWO

The Hospital

Fourteen

•

When Wentik regained consciousness, his first impulse was one of panic.

He was in darkness, and a high-pitched whining noise ran on interminably around him.

He tried to move, but found that his entire body was confined by a heavy garment which allowed him no movement other than a slight sideways rolling. A rubber mask covered his nose and mouth, and cool air was being pumped along it, tending to counter the surge of claustrophobia that had at first swelled in him.

His return to full awareness was swift, and left him with remarkably few after-effects. Only a slight ache across the top of his forehead remained to remind him of the acrid yellow gas.

Within minutes he had steadied himself, and lay calmly where he was. Although events were now beyond his control, he felt instinctively that he was in no immediate danger.

After twenty minutes, a man came in carrying a bowl of hot liquid. He placed it on the floor in front of Wentik, and backed away towards the door through which he had come.

Wentik wriggled violently, and tried to speak through the mask.

The man looked at him, reached outside the door, and lights came on. Wentik rolled his eyes meaningfully at the food, and tried again to get words out.

The man pulled him to a sitting position, and fiddled around with some strings behind him. Wentik's hands came free. He looked down at them, and realized that he was inside a kind of strait-jacket.

The man went out.

Wentik pulled the bowl towards him, and loosened the rubber mask from around his mouth. It was connected, by way of flexible rubber tubes, to two gas-cylinders lying on the floor.

Wentik took off the mask, breathed the air in the chamber, and found it to be perfectly acceptable. He wondered for a moment why he had been put inside the mask.

The soup was very hot, and highly spiced. It seemed to have a basic stock of meat extract with an admixture of chopped vegetables and bread. The taste was unusual and not altogether pleasant, but Wentik drank it in minutes and felt better when he had finished.

When the man had gone out of the chamber he had left the door partially open, and Wentik climbed to his feet and went to it. In front of him was another chamber, equipped with two bunks and washing and cooking facilities. Here, the whining noise was less.

In the centre of the floor was the now-familiar set of gas-cylinders, and on one of the bunks lay Musgrove. Wentik walked over and looked at him.

He was bound in a strait-jacket, and his mouth and nose were covered with a rubber mask. He looked up at Wentik, his eyes revealing a passive interest.

Wentik moved to take off the mask, but just at that moment the first man came in through a door at the far end of the chamber.

'Get back,' he said at once.

Wentik looked at him.

'Why's Musgrove bound up like that?' he said.

'It's for his own good. Now get back.'

Wentik looked down again at Musgrove, then walked slowly into the chamber in which he'd come round. He deliberately left the door open, and watched the man check the rubber straps which held the mask around Musgrove's face. When he was satisfied that Wentik had not disturbed them, he returned to the far chamber.

As the door opened and closed, Wentik saw into it and his suspicions were confirmed. It was the cockpit of an aircraft. He was on the VTOL jet.

Which meant he was being taken somewhere. And Musgrove

too, though where the man had come from and how he had appeared at the jail with the pilot of the aircraft was a mystery.

For those few brief seconds, when he'd seen Musgrove by the helicopter, the man had seemed to be working with the other. Yet now he was a strait-jacketed prisoner, like himself.

There was an almost inaudible change in the pitch of the whining noise, so subtle that as soon as he had detected it, Wentik doubted that it had changed at all. He assumed that behind the rear wall of this chamber were the engines. It was surprising how much space there was inside the craft, considering the apparent size of it from the outside.

A voice crackled in through a concealed speaker.

'Preparing to land. Take safety precautions.'

Wentik looked round, and saw a short row of double belts hanging from the wall. He went over, hooked his arms through one set, and felt them tighten automatically against his shoulders. He braced his legs against the floor, uncertain of how securely he needed to be buffered against the rigours of landing.

Almost at once the pitch of the engines changed again, and noise flooded in from the compartment. The front of the craft lifted, and Wentik felt a kind of swooping motion, presumably as the craft executed a similar manoeuvre to the one it had done when it stopped in front of the helicopter. His stomach lurched as he felt the machine drop, and he realized the need for everyone on board to be strapped down. Twice more the plane swooped, then Wentik heard a combination of noises: the engines taking on a newer, harsher pitch, and a rattling scraping noise, like the anchor-chains of a ship.

After three minutes of this there was a sideways movement, the nose of the aircraft dropped suddenly and the noise of the engines dwindled away to inaudibility.

Wentik stayed where he was, unsure of what he should do.

He unlooped his arms from the straps, and tried to get the heavy garment from around his body. Although his fingers were free, the stiffness of the material prevented him from moving his arms anywhere behind his back other than at one angle, and try as he might he wasn't able to find any way of undoing the stays. He struggled for about five minutes, then abandoned it.

The continuing silence from the rest of the aircraft puzzled him. Why hadn't the men come down for him?

After waiting several more minutes, Wentik moved into the next chamber again. Musgrove still lay there, his eyes closed.

Wentik went across to him, and lifted the rubber mask away from his mouth.

The man's eyes opened.

'Wentik!'he said.

'Are you all right?' His face was covered in a slimy mixture of perspiration and grime.

He closed his eyes and opened them again.

'I'm OK. Have we landed?'

'Yes. Where are we, Musgrove?'

'I don't know.' The man sat up, and caught Wentik's arm. 'Listen, you've got to get me away from here. I only took them to you because I was forced to. We should escape together.'

Wentik looked uncertainly at him. He had grown to distrust Musgrove's sanity for obvious reasons.

It disturbed Wentik to realize that the people who had tied him up had likewise strait-jacketed Musgrove.

He said: 'Let's find where we are before trying to escape.'

He walked past the man to the end of the cabin. Here the door was closed, and he opened it slowly. The cockpit was deserted.

Sunlight shone in brightly through one of the large screens in the sides, and fell across rows of dials and instruments. There were two padded seats by each of the screens, and flying controls. Wentik looked briefly at the instruments, but they meant little to him.

In the floor of the cockpit was a large metal hatch, which had been opened. A short ladder led down to the ground. Wentik knelt in the cumbersome strait-jacket and tried to see if anyone was about, but there was no one in the immediate vicinity.

Standing up again, he looked through the screens and saw that the aircraft had been landed on an expanse of concrete. There were several other aircraft nearby of different sizes.

He went back to the hatch, and climbed down the ladder.

The sun was dropping down towards low hills on the horizon, in that blaze of orange and red light that indicates an industrial atmosphere. In minutes it would be dark. Wentik looked around at the airport, trying to sort out some order from the mass of unfamiliar shapes and colours.

There were about twenty or thirty aircraft dotted about the port, which, for its apparent density of traffic, was surprisingly small. If, as he expected, all the aircraft used vertical take-off, then this of course would explain the seeming anomaly. Dozens of people moved about the craft, none of them taking any notice of him.

About five hundred yards from where he was standing there was a tall terminal-building, and across its face was written:

SAO PAULO

So that was where he was. One of the largest cities in Brazil, from what he could recall. For what seemed like the hundredth time, Wentik wished ruefully that his knowledge of Brazil were greater.

As he looked around, wondering what he should do next, a vehicle came across the concrete, stopped a few yards away from him, and two men climbed out.

They came across to him.

'Have you just come here in that?' one of them said, nodding towards the aircraft.

Wentik said: 'Yes.'

'All right. Climb in.'

They went back to the vehicle, and Wentik followed them, looking at it curiously. At the front were two seats for the driver and his companion, and in the back was a simple padded couch that could evidently double as a seat or a bed.

The whole vehicle was open.

He said: 'You want me to get in that?'

The man said: 'It's up to you. You don't look too sick to me. You don't have to lie down.'

'What is this, an ambulance?'

'That's right. We can opaque it, if you'd prefer.'

He moved a switch in the front of the vehicle, and at once the whole of the rear became surrounded by a pale blue oval cocoon that seemed to materialize from the molecules of the air. Wentik put his hand against it. It was soft.

He climbed into the back and sat down, as the man had suggested, on the side of the bunk. He could see through the cocoon quite clearly. Its purpose was evident: to give privacy to those who required it, and yet allow whoever was inside to see out.

The vehicle moved away, with no sound of a motor. As they rolled towards the side of the terminal-building, a jet on the far side of the airport started its engine, and the whole area was submerged in a torrent of sound. The plane took off in seconds, climbing vertically into the sky in a deafening blast of noise.

By the time the air had quietened again they were out of the airport, and driving along a narrow street. Wentik had been aware of a strange sensation ever since he had stepped out of the aircraft, and now he identified it.

People.

For the first time in weeks he was surrounded by more people than he could count. Even before he had left the Concentration he had been in a closed, confined community, where each face was as familiar as the rest. Now he saw thousands of human beings, dressed in a multitude of different colours. Here were jostling crowds on narrow pavements, children darting across the street in front of the traffic. And women.

Wentik realized how long it was since he had seen any women.

The ambulance was forced to slow in the street as the throng overflowed from the pavements. They were passing through a kind of market, with open stalls containing fruit and vegetables, bread, wine, unidentifiable objects in shining metals and colourful plastics. The stallholders were closing the stalls down, transferring their wares to nearby trucks. Night was approaching.

On the walls of the buildings brilliant, lighted signs flashed in the growing shade. Looking down the street in the direction they were heading, over the heads of the men in the front of the vehicle, Wentik saw the street as a path through a forest of colour. His eyes, long accustomed to the simple bleakness of the jail and the plain, and abstract of light and dark, saw the signs not as individual blazes of light, but as part of an overall kaleidoscope.

And when he looked at some of the signs, their strangeness was immediately apparent.

Here a sign showed a handful of flowers, there a face. An over-simplified drawing of scissors, the face of a woman, fish, an open book. Nowhere did he see any words.

Gradually, the street widened and the ambulance picked up speed. Now the buildings weren't so close together, and took on a more pleasing sense of design. The sun had disappeared, leaving a broad fan of ebbing colour in the sky. Lights were coming on in the buildings and Wentik, experiencing a renewed sense of imprisonment in the shell of the ambulance, felt desolated and apart from the people of this city. Here they were going through their normal routines: living, relaxing, loving and making love. But he was no part of it; an intruder in a strait-jacket driven discreetly through darkening streets to an unknown destination.

The buildings started to cluster again, and the ambulance slowed a little. The coloured signs were not to be seen. The vehicle left the main road and followed a circuitous route through lesser streets where high blocks rose into the evening sky, their windows ablaze with light.

Wentik looked around with interest, subjectively still only minutes away from the jail.

Suddenly the vehicle braked, and turned into the courtyard of a long building. Bright arc-lamps came on as they drove around to the back, and light flooded around them as they stopped. The two men jumped down at once, and the light seemed to grow even brighter. Then Wentik realized that the blue, sheltering cocoon had disappeared.

He climbed down, and the men each took one of his arms, gripping him firmly by the straps sewn into the fabric of the jacket behind his triceps.

Powerless, Wentik was propelled up a flight of stairs, and into a tiled hall where their footsteps clattered loudly.

Before he had a chance to absorb the scene in the hall – a frenzied glance at a crowd of people, some standing, some sitting, all seeming to be waiting – he was through, and into a corridor.

Halfway along he was thrust into a lift, and taken up and up. Wentik found himself counting the floors, stopping at seven.

They took him along another corridor, through a complex of rooms, and into another passage. At the end of this they opened a door, and let him through.

One of the men slipped a catch just beneath his neck, and the strait-jacket fell forward and off. Wentik instinctively flexed the muscles of his shoulders, and turned round. He looked at the men.

'Where am I?' he said.

One of the men slipped a tattered piece of card from a pocket and read from it.

'You're in São Paulo,' he read in a monotone. 'This is a hospital. Make yourself comfortable, get as much sleep as possible, and do what is requested of you by the medical staff. There will be a nurse along to look after you in a moment.'

He returned it to the pocket, and both men moved towards the door.

The other one said: 'And don't try to get out. You'll never make it.'

The door shut, and Wentik heard the lock click into place. The men walked away down the corridor. He looked around the room.

It was light, and pleasantly decorated. There was a bed – with sheets, Wentik observed at once – a row of books, a wash-basin with soap and towels, a wardrobe, a desk and a chair, and a change of clothing laid out for him on the bed. Compared with what he had grown accustomed to over the last few weeks, it was luxury.

Ten minutes later, when he had washed and changed into the clothes provided for him – a grey, close-fitting tee-shirt and seamless, loose-fitting trousers, also grey – he noticed that the walls of the room were padded with resilient fibre.

Fifteen

•

An hour later, Wentik lay on the top of the bed, listening to gentle music piped in through a loudspeaker concealed above the door, and watching a film of children playing happily in a meadow under blue skies. In a curious parallel between this and his early days at the jail, the vague questioning he had just undergone had left him in a state of mild confusion.

A young doctor had visited him, and the questions he asked had been virtually meaningless to Wentik.

And, apparently, the answers he had given meant just as little to the doctor.

There followed a perfunctory medical examination, and he was left in peace.

It seemed to be a case of mistaken identity, as far as Wentik could tell. The doctor thought he was someone else, though precisely who wasn't clear. Part of the examination had included simple association tests, and Wentik's responses had evidently surprised the doctor.

At the end of the examination, Wentik had said: 'Why have I been brought here?'

'For disturbance rehabilitation.'

'How long does it last?'

'Until you recover,' the doctor said. 'Call the nurse if you want anything. I'll see you again in the morning.'

When he went out, the door was not re-locked and Wentik opened it a fraction. A desk had been placed in the corridor outside, and a temporary partition erected, thus effectively converting the end of the corridor into an outer room to his own. Sitting at the desk was a nurse dressed in a white uniform.. The doctor had paused, and exchanged a few words with her. Although he strained his hearing to its utmost, Wentik had been unable to distinguish most of what was said.

Though he did hear Musgrove's name mentioned once by the doctor.

When the doctor left, he stood for several seconds watching the nurse at her work. Unaware of his scrutiny, she bent her head over her writing. She was young, and to Wentik's eyes long starved of feminine features, remarkably attractive. Finally, realizing he was doing no good to his state of mind, he had closed the door silently, and gone back to the bed.

Within minutes, the lights had dimmed of their own accord, and the film started.

It was entirely innocuous, seeming to be a kind of travelogue without commentary. All the scenes were of absolute simplicity: broad white beaches with rolling surf, tall mountains in a mantle of dark-green trees and edged with white cloud, faces of men and women, children playing, animals feeding, factory chimneys smoking.

And meanwhile, the insipid, innocuous music trickled in through the speaker into the room.

After an hour of the film the lights came on again, the music stopped and the door opened. The nurse came in.

'Would you get undressed please, Mr Musgrove?' she said.

'Musgrove?'

'Yes. And I'll bring you a drink before you go to sleep.'

She went out again before Wentik could say anything.

She had called him Musgrove. Was that who they thought he was? He thought back, and realized that from the time he had climbed out of the VTOL aircraft he had spoken to no one beyond the ambulance men. If they had been instructed to pick up a man from the aircraft – and both he and Musgrove had been wearing similar clothes, even down to the strait-jacket – then mistaken identity could easily have followed.

In which case he was receiving treatment evidently designed for a man in Musgrove's condition, and not for his. While being immediately comforting, it gave him an added insight into the man.

When the nurse came back with a mug of hot tea, he said to her: 'Who do you think I am, nurse?'

She put down the drink, and straightened his bedclothes.

'Now you get that drink inside you, and go to sleep, Mr Musgrove.'

'You didn't answer my question.'

She smiled at him, and Wentik's heart quickened.

'Go to sleep. The doctor will see you in the morning.'

She moved to the door, and went back outside. Wentik swung his legs out of the sheets and, using his recent discovery that the door could be opened without making a noise, peered at her. God, she was pretty!

She looked up and smiled.

'I said go to sleep, Mr Musgrove.'

He shut the door quickly.

It no longer seemed to matter who she thought he was. He got back into bed, drank his tea as soon as it was sufficiendy cool, and within minutes was asleep.

It is a part of human thought to rationalize, being the one attribute of man that sets him apart from the other primates. In any given set of circumstances a man can use the information he has available to form an hypothesis which he can then or later set out to establish as workable or unworkable. Man as an individual had been able to experiment upon himself; using his known environments as first postulates he had gradually worked his rationalizing process to invent society, and art and culture. And war and megadeaths, prejudice and hatred.

Frighten a man, starve him, freeze him or burn him – if he knows who he is and where he is and what is happening to him, he will retain his power to rationalize. But deprive him of this, and he becomes something less than human.

As he had grown accustomed to doing at the jail, Wentik awoke early the next morning, and lay in his bed fighting to rationalize his situation.

He knew what had happened to him, but he didn't know why. He knew about a mechanical hand that sprouted from the top of a table, but he didn't know how. He could accept the presence of a computer in a disused building, but what was its precise function? He could understand a field-generator that somehow invoked a kind of temporal upheaval, but he couldn't think why.

And he could understand a case of mistaken identity, but he didn't see a way out of it.

Wentik fought for rationalism, but it was beginning to reject him.

He had been awake about an hour before the nurse came in to attend to him. He turned to face her as she came in, then saw that the pretty one had evidently gone off duty to be replaced by a round-faced plump woman of middle age.

'Good morning, Mr Musgrove,' she said cheerfully. 'What would you like for breakfast?'

Breakfast. He had forgotten that such a concept existed. Food was food and didn't have names.

'Er – just coffee, please,' he said uncertainly.

'Nothing else?'

'No. That is, unless you have some fruit?' She smiled again.

'Of course. I'll see what I can find.'

She touched a button set into a wall, and a part of it turned away like slats in a Venetian blind. Sunshine poured in, and Wentik screwed up his eyes against the unexpected influx of light.

The nurse went out again, and as soon as she had disappeared through the outer office, Wentik climbed quickly from the bed, washed rapidly and pulled on his new clothes.

He went into the outer office and, finding a key in his door, removed it and pocketed it. To his left now was a desk with several papers scattered upon it, a clock, a pen and pencil, and a textbook. He picked it up. It was called: *Netchik's Revised Psychotherapeutics.*

Through the glass upper-half of the partition he could see the whole length of the corridor. It was deserted. He crossed to the other door, and turned the handle.

It was locked.

He rattled it, but it wouldn't budge. Deeply frustrated, he returned to his room, and sat down on the bed.

While he was waiting for his breakfast, he went across to the bookshelf and looked at the titles there. He scanned them quickly. With few exceptions the books appeared to be light novels. He pulled one or two of them down. The first was a romance which, according to a discreet blurb on the cover, was the story of a young woman's career as an air-hostess on a transcontinental jet. Another was a 'fearless document of depravity' in a Rio slum. Wentik's eyebrows raised; strong stuff for a hospital bedside bookshelf. A third one he looked at was an adventure set in the 'new Amazonian frontier'.

At the end of the row was a slim book entitled: *Brazil – Concise Social History*.

Wentik pulled it out and opened the cover. On the fly was the imprint: 'Luiz de Sequeira SA, São Paulo 2178'.

Just then, the nurse came back carrying a large tray. She put it down on the table, and took a metal cover off a plate. Underneath, fried kidneys and boiled rice awaited his attention. There was a tall jug of coffee next to this, and a bowl of oranges, tangerines and bananas. The nurse lifted off the bowl, and put it to one side. Wentik's eyes then really opened. Behind the bowl had been concealed a small dish of fresh strawberries.

'Where the devil do you get these from?' he asked incredulously.

'It's all local produce. Would you like a mango?'

Wentik considered.

'Yes. I've never tried one before.'

The nurse saw the book he was holding.

'Good, I'm glad you've started on the reading. You've got to get through all of them before we let you out,' she added archly.

'The whole lot?'

She nodded.

'It's part of the course.'

'Where is the doctor, as a matter of interest?'

'He'll be coming in to see you this morning. In about two hours.' She tapped her finger on the edge of his plate. 'Your kidneys will get cold.'

She walked out of the door, and closed it behind her. Wentik watched her go. Certainly she was more forthcoming than the pretty one, but he knew which of the two he'd prefer to have around him. What time, he wondered, did the other one come back on duty?

He sat down at the table, pulled the plate of kidneys towards him, took a mouthful, and opened the book.

As he ate, he started skimming through it quickly.

The book was not really much more than an extended essay. It began with the discovery of the 'island' of Santa Cruz by Pedro Alvares Cabral in 1500, at the start of the great years of Portuguese colonialism. The story continued with fresh discoveries, as the Portuguese slowly began to realize the magnitude of their new real estate. Wentik skipped through this part of the book quickly, not concerned with what, to him, was common history.

He read of the downfall of the colonial rule, and the setting up of the Brazilian Empire, and here the Brazilian society began to take on its own character.

The agricultural regions of the north-east, semi-nomadic and existing on a flimsy basis of slave labour; the attempts to conquer and exploit the mighty wasteland of the Amazonia; the discovery of raw materials, vast deposits of quartz, zinc, coal, iron and gold, and the setting-up of the industrial complex along the south-easterly shores; the growth of the coffee industry in the south and the emergence of the rubber-barons in the north.

And he read too of the gradual domination of the native, and the influx of immigrants from the whole world: Japan, Europe, Australia, India, Turkey and North America. How the few families, representing less than one per cent of the entire nation, owned more than half its wealth. And as the Empire fell, and the Brazilian Republic was formed, how the social problems arose: disease, poverty and crime. Gradually the Republic slipped into the hands of the military until the late twentieth century, the 1960s and 1970s, when martial law was the only kind there was.

All this was vaguely familiar to Wentik. He hadn't exacdy studied the history of Brazil in the past, but items of news trickled into his knowledge via the media of television and newspaper reports.

Brazil, long one of the stablest of the South American countries, had been sliding into military dictatorship ever since the beginning of the twentieth century.

Wentik turned the page.

The next section was headed: 'Post-War Reformation'. Wentik had to read the words twice before he made sense of them.

He took a few more mouthfuls of food, and went on. In three barren paragraphs, Wentik learned about the Third World War.

Using precise and economical English, the anonymous writer related a series of incidents which to him were old cold history and which to Wentik were something akin to divine revelation. The writer was talking about 1989 as if it had hardly existed, yet to Wentik it was of now. The day he had left the Concentration was 19th May 1989, and only a few subjective weeks had elapsed since.

In July 1989, according to the writer, the first stage of the war took place when the post-revolutionary Cuban society invaded the south-eastern tip of the United States. The purpose of the war was not stated, though Wentik could remember reading somewhere about the rapidly fraying political tempers between the two countries. For eight incredible days, the tiny force of Cubans, representing virtually the whole of the country's armed forces, had fought their way three hundred miles up the Florida peninsula. Cape Canaveral had fallen to them, and the space-centre destroyed. Finally, in a massive counter-attack, in which the Americans had used almost every kind of weapon available to them, the invasion force had been wiped out. The first-ever invasion of the American continent had been launched ... and repulsed.

A week later the inevitable reprisals were carried out, and the cities of Havana and Manzanillo were H-bombed.

Within days the international diplomatic climate had deteriorated, and the communist bloc declared war on the United States. By the end of the year, the war was over. The book was infuriatingly vague about details ... the actual stages of the war not being delineated, only the results.

There followed a period the historian called The Trucial Years, but Wentik assumed this was a euphemism for chaos.

In 2043 an aerial survey team was commissioned by the Australian government to survey those parts of the world with which there had been no communication. Their report was made public in 2055.

Almost the whole of the North American continent had been razed by nuclear bombing. Much of Western Europe, the same, though parts of Spain and Portugal had escaped the bombing and atmospheric radiation was low. Most Communist cities had been destroyed, though there were large areas of Russia undamaged by blast. India and the Far East had escaped most of the bombing, but what fall-out had not done to the population, famine and drought had. Africa was lightly damaged, but had reverted to inter-tribal violence; black anarchy was the norm. Australia, badly shattered by the bombing, was recovering, and rebuilding her cities, though the spirit of the people was crushed.

Only the South American continent had gone untouched by bombing, and had suffered lightest from radiation.

But then, said the writer, the Disturbances had begun. This time, South America did not escape.

In their own way, the Disturbances did more permanent damage to the world than the bombing. Cities were wrecked, wars flared up over petty issues, whole ideologies crumbled. There were no euphemisms here, the writer describing each of the major effects of the Disturbances in detail. Much of it was lost on Wentik, names he did not know, places unfamiliar to him.

Whatever happened, and whatever may have caused the Disturbances, it was plain that the writer treated the matter with the utmost gravity.

Now came the era of the Reformation.

In the last years of the twenty-first century the Disturbances had lost much of their effect, and social order was restored. Again, South America, and Brazil in particular, was quickest to recover. The whole continent joined in a massive re-allocation of land and resources. During the Disturbances there had been immigration to Brazil of all those people capable of getting there, and the country was a mixing-pot of races. Now it was divided up into new nations, with each representative interest claiming and receiving self-determination.

The change had taken nearly thirty years to bring to conclusion, yet when it was settled it was seen to be working, and had gone on doing so ever since.

The native Brazilians settled mainly in the extreme north-east, reverting to the farmlands they had worked before the coming of the Portuguese. There was a large and vociferous Jewish community, and they had settled in and around Manaus, their new Promised Land a frontier of river, swamps and rain-forest. And in the south, with the rebuilt São Paulo as the centre, the immigrant English-speaking peoples had congregated.

In practice, the writer pointed out, the living and working conditions were effectively different from the broad basics that this might imply. Only in São Paulo was there a predominance of Caucasian stock. In most cities, from Porto Alegre in the south to Belem in the north, there was the traditionally Brazilian intermingling of races, cheerfully independent of each other, yet each respectful of the others' rights.

And each state respected the others. Brazil was now too heavily populated and just too physically large for effective centralized government. When self-determination was established, that was exactly what was achieved. Each community had clear boundaries, and within those the local government ruled as it pleased.

The last section of the book was an extended ideological plan, taking in the planned increase of food-production and birth-rate over the next few years, the gradual expansion into previously uninhabitable areas of the globe, and finally the establishment of a world unity.

Wentik closed the book, and realized that beyond a few mouthfuls he had not eaten his breakfast. He ate the remaining pieces of meat although they had grown cold, and poured himself a cup of coffee. He drank this and had just poured himself a second cup when the nurse came in.

'Have you finished, Mr Musgrove?'

'I wonder if I could keep a few pieces of fruit?'

'Of course.'

She lifted up the tray, left the strawberries on the table, and walked to the door.

He said to her: 'When does your shift finish, nurse?'

'We do three shifts of eight hours each. I'm on until four this afternoon, then Nurse Dawson takes over.'

'I see. Thank you.'

She went out and shut the door, and Wentik started on the strawberries.

He thought back over what he had read, trying to assimilate it. That the world he had known and lived in no longer existed was too much to grasp. Particularly when the nature of its destruction was related in concise summary form, as if it were a part of common knowledge.

Nuclear warfare was a potentiality of which everyone of his time was aware, yet it was inconceivable in practice. One could comprehend the gradual kind of destruction, where one army would systematically dismantle the country of another, or bomb it, or vandalize it by their presence. But a series of worldwide nuclear explosions, capable of killing millions of people in seconds, was something no mind could fully imagine.

Yet ... it seemed to have happened. Unless everything he was now experiencing was some dreadful illusion, he was sitting here in a city called São Paulo in a year numbered 2189.

He went cold inside.

Jean was dead. And the children.

Western Europe destroyed, the book had said. He grabbed it, and found the page. '... with the exception of the south-western corner of the Spanish peninsula, Western and Central Europe were laid waste in the second wave of nuclear bombings ... '

No dates. No damned dates in the book.

Wentik looked along the shelf containing the remainder of the books, but could find nothing that might contain a reference to the war. He went back to the table and sat down.

The true bleakness of his situation now struck him. Just as the day before he had found that he could accept he was in a future time, so he now comprehended the awful isolation of it. Even could he get back to his own time, it would do no good. The war was an historical certainty. As was the death of his family.

He rested his elbows on the table, and leaned his head forward, so that the heels of his hands pressed against his eyes. Presently he felt the bitter warmth of tears trickle down the inside of his forearms.

Sixteen

•

Later that morning the doctor visited him.

Wentik was sitting at the table, reading one of the books. It was the least whimsical one he could find, about a cattle-rancher in the hills behind Rio Grande whose stock was beset by an unidentifiable blight. As a piece of fiction it was unexciting in the extreme, but he felt he would prefer it to the romantic entanglements of an air-hostess.

The doctor came into the room without knocking.

He said: 'Now, Mr Musgrove. How do you feel?'

'I feel fine,' Wentik said. 'And I'd like to set one thing straight. My name is not Musgrove, but Wentik. Doctor Elias Wentik. I want to be discharged.'

The doctor looked at his notes uncertainly.

'I see. Could you spell that for me?'

Wentik obliged him, then said: 'When do I leave?'

'I'm afraid we can't discharge you. You're not fully rehabilitated yet.' He wrote hurriedly on a piece of paper. 'I want you to read as much as you can, and we'll show you some more films this evening. You've got to concentrate on them, do you understand? They're most important.'

Wentik nodded.

'Now then,' the doctor said. 'Is there anything else you'd like?'

Wentik replied: 'I'd like a clock.'

'Yes, yes. You shall have one. I really meant, something more – how can I put it? – *abstract?* Companionable?'

'I don't know what you mean.'

'Never mind. Is there anything else?'

'Could you tell me the date, please?' The doctor glanced at his wristwatch. 'The fifteenth.'

'Of what?'

'February. Er – 2189.'

'Thank you. Look, doctor, there's been a mistake. I know you think I'm a man called Musgrove, but I'm not. My name is Wentik. Elias Wentik. I came here on a plane with Musgrove, and I think I was picked up by your ambulance men in mistake for Musgrove.'

The doctor said: 'I see.'

'Well,' Wentik demanded. 'Don't you believe me?'

'Can you prove this yourself?'

'I don't think so. Unless Musgrove was found at the airport.'

'Well, I'm sorry.'

The doctor opened the door.

'I'll see if I can find out anything for you. But you'll have to stay here until then.'

He shut the door in evident confusion, and for several seconds Wentik stood just looking at the closed door.

It would be nice to get out of here, if only so that he could exercise a little freedom of will once again. Other than this, he had no positive reason to leave. He had no idea of why he had been brought to São Paulo, nor who was responsible. If it was Musgrove then it was very peculiar, since he seemed to be at present occupying the position that had been set aside for him. From all appearances, this was a kind of detentive therapy that set out to rehabilitate its patients, though from what to what Wentik was at a loss to see. In which case it could be assumed that Musgrove was in need of it, and therefore was not in complete control of his movements.

For Wentik to escape now would not be totally impossible. With one female guard and a thin partition, he wouldn't have much difficulty in getting away. It was a hospital, after all, and not a prison. Little details like keys left in doors seemed to indicate that the detention in cases like this was often voluntary.

Wentik went back to his desk, and rejoined the problems of the cattle-rancher.

*

After a meal had been brought to him in the evening, and the tray had been taken away, Wentik relaxed on his bed in preparation for the films to start. Anything would be a break from the tiresome reading that was his only diversion.

He had finished the cattle-rancher book before lunch, and after the meal read the history of Brazil again.

The nurse brought the clock for him after his lunch, and immediately he felt better. At four o'clock he had heard the nurses change shifts, and soon after verified that the young one was on duty. He wondered momentarily what his unseen guardian, the one on the midnight to eight o'clock shift, was like.

But the day dragged with almost intolerable slowness.

He ate a lot of the fruit and, against his better judgment, read the air-hostess book. It was as bad as he had anticipated, the only virtue in it being the eventual sacrifice of the girl's virginity to the villain of the piece.

Sunset was a long time coming, and the orange halations against the edge of the branch outside his window stayed visible for nearly half an hour. Finally they dimmed away, and the sky turned rapidly from a dark blue to a black.

He pressed the button in the wall, and the slat-like window blinds turned, again forming part of the white-painted wall.

Before returning to the bed, he opened the door a fraction and looked at the girl sitting at her desk. The name-tag sewn across the sleeve of her blouse said: *Nse Karena Dawson.* She gave no sign that she knew he was looking at her, but after a few seconds a slow blush spread across her cheeks. He moved away again quietly, and sat on the edge of the bed.

Minutes passed, and the film didn't seem to be starting.

Outside he heard Nurse Dawson's chair squeak against the wooden flooring as she stood up. He heard her lift a phone and dial it.

Round the edge of the door, he saw her standing with her back to him, speaking quickly and quietly into the receiver. She put it down, then folded her arms and stood still, as if waiting.

Curiously, Wentik stood back a little way from the door, restricting his view somewhat but ensuring she wouldn't see him.

After about five minutes there was a noise, and a second nurse came into the outer office. The two girls spoke together very quietly, the second one nodding occasionally.

Wentik went back to the bed, and sat down. Whatever was going on probably involved him, and he would doubtiess find out in due course what it was.

He waited for less than two minutes when the nurse came into the room. Wentik noticed that the slight blush had returned to her face.

She said: 'The films will start in a minute. I thought I would come and explain what some of the scenes are about.'

She closed the door, and said to him in a much softer voice: ' Do you have the key to this?'

He nodded and passed it over. She took it from him and, with hands that trembled slightly, locked it. When she was sure it was secure, she came over to the bed.

'Anna owes me a favour,' she said. 'And I thought I'd take advantage of it.'

Just then the fights dimmed, and the film began. Wentik looked at it quickly, and saw that it was the same one as last night.

'What are you doing here?' he said.

'Keeping you company, of course.'

'Should you be here?' She laughed.

'No. At least, not if you were who they thought you were.'

'You mean they know I'm not Musgrove?'

'They do now. They're going to discharge you in the morning. You weren't to be told yet.'

'Why not?'

She shrugged.

'I don't know. You might as well stay here as anywhere, I suppose.'

Wentik glanced at the part of the wall on to which the film was being projected.

'I don't need to watch that then?'

She shook her head, and said: 'That was just an excuse. I didn't tell Anna exactly why I came in.'

'Why did you then?'

She said: 'Move up.'

He obliged, and she sat down on the bed next to him. 'I told you, I thought you'd like some company.'

'You're quite perceptive.'

'Are you married, Doctor Wentik?' she said.

He looked at her ... confronted for the first time with a new factor of his life. 'No,' he said slowly. 'My wife's no longer alive.'

'I'm sorry.'

He put his arm hesitantly around her shoulders. 'You're very attractive,' he said.

She said nothing, but laid her hand on his leg.

And then he kissed her, and she responded at once. His hand fell naturally against her breast, and she pushed her body against him. Their kissing grew more passionate, and he pulled her down beside him on to the bed.

Behind them, on the wall, the meaningless colour pictures flickered their homely message. Perhaps Anna hadn't been told everything, but at least she had the sense not to pipe in the music.

Seventeen

•

Wentik was still asleep the following morning when the middle-aged nurse brought in his breakfast. She pressed the button on the wall and sunshine flooded into the room. Wentik opened his eyes, and saw the branch of blossom outside his window. Pink blossom, and innocent.

She put down the tray on the table and walked out quickly.

He lay where he was for two minutes more, trying to restore wakefulness to his body. His muscles felt disconnected from his limbs. Already the comforts and vices of civilization were sapping his energy. The jail, for all its stark unpleasantness, had restored a vigour to his movements that he had not known since his adolescence.

He got out of bed at last, and pulled the tray towards him. No kidneys today, he saw. A simple bowl of cereal, a fried egg and coffee.

When he had finished, he washed and dressed, attempted to pull the bedclothes back into a semblance of tidiness, and sat back to await developments.

Karena had said that as far as she knew he was to be discharged this morning. The hospital were embarrassed about what had happened.

The clock showed the time of ten-thirty and Wentik was beginning to get bored again, when there was a knock on the door and the nurse came in. Behind her was a tall man who strode over to him at once.

'Doctor Wentik! How sorry I am this has happened to you!'

Wentik took the proffered hand, and shook it. He looked at the other man.

He was elderly, probably in his late sixties, though still upright in bearing and with clear, intelligent eyes. He was almost bald, with traces of white hair at his temples. Although his face was wrinkled, his features were solid and his skin a healthy pink. He was wearing similar clothes to Wentik's new ones; comfortable, close-fitting and a neutral grey in colour. Over his shoulders he wore a bright, lime-green cape.

Wentik said: 'I haven't had the pleasure.'

'Jexon. Samuel Jexon.'

They carried on shaking each other's hand. The newcomer's manner seemed to be one of reunion, or as if he had been waiting for some time to meet Wentik.

Finally, he said: 'If you can put your things together, I'll take you down to your apartment.'

'I'm ready to go now.'

'Don't you have any change of clothes with you?'

'No, only these that the nurse gave me. My others are almost unwearable now.'

'But I thought you'd bring some.'

'I did. But they got lost on the way.'

'I'll see what I can do for you then. I've got a plane outside. Your apartment is in the same building as my office, and I can get some of the students to find you something.'

'Students?'

'At the university.'

Wentik picked up the history book, and followed Jexon into the corridor. The plump nurse glanced at him as he passed through her office, and he could detect that her friendly oudook of the day before had gone by the board. Almost as if now she had found that he wasn't the real Musgrove, and thus was in no need of her care and attention, she resented his presence.

Jexon walked with an unmistakable air of authority through the building, with Wentik on his heels.

At one point Wentik said in a wry voice: 'Don't I get a strait-jacket this time?'

'Who did that to you?' Jexon said with a pained expression. 'Was it Musgrove?'

'I think so. I was given a heavy sedative, and came round tied up inside one.'

'You'll have to accept my apology, Doctor Wentik. Tell me about anything else like that. I was the one who had you brought here.'

They came out into the sunlight at the rear of the building, where the ambulance had stopped two nights before. On the concrete was a small, green-painted aircraft with a high, bulbous cockpit squatting cumbersomely atop a narrow fuselage.

Wentik stopped dead.

'You brought me here,' he repeated.

'That's right.'

'Tell me just one thing. *Why?*'

Jexon pointed to the book Wentik was holding.

'If you've read that, you'll already know a part of the answer.'

'I didn't learn much from it. Only that there has been a war.'

'There has been a war,' Jexon said in a gently mocking tone. 'The war to end all wars, I'm afraid. That used to be an ironic saying in your time, I believe. Well, they meant it. It didn't just blow half the world to pieces, it broke man's spirit. Do you realize it's taken us two hundred years to get to where we are now? It probably all looks strange to you, but we haven't got many things now that you didn't have. We've caught up with you, Doctor Wentik, that's all.'

'But you didn't get me here just because of a war.'

'Partly we did.' Jexon nodded towards the aircraft. 'Come on. Get in. I think you'll understand why when I can explain a few things.'

They climbed up into the aircraft, and sat down. Jexon placed himself before a set of controls that to Wentik's uninitiated eye looked no more complicated than those of a private car.

The ambiguity of Jexon's last statement still hovered in his mind.

'You say you've caught up with me?' he said. 'Partly because of the war?'

The man laughed.

'Not you personally. Your society. We're rebuilding a civilization here. Our level of technology is just about what it was in your time. In some ways, in the social sciences, we're ahead of you, and in some technical respects. But overall, the way of life here is not greatly different from yours.'

Wentik realized that while the man had been talking, the plane had taken off, and they were now about twenty feet from the ground and rising quickly in total silence. He looked down through the wide canopy and saw the city spreading out below him. The day was clear and warm, the sky a transparent blue. The overall aspect of the city was one of space. It abounded in tall buildings, concrete and metal constructions not unlike those Wentik had grown accustomed to in his own time. But they didn't cluster on each other, they were well spaced with patches of greenery. Towards the outskirts of the city, the buildings weren't so tall, yet even here the natural green of trees and shrubbery abounded.

Jexon said: 'Do you like it?'

Wentik nodded, but added: 'It's not like home.'

'Where is that?'

'London.'

'I thought you were an American.

'No.'

Wentik looked across the city to the hills beyond. It really was a beautiful place, if the heat was discounted. In the other direction he could see the sea, the South Adantic, as a strip of silver along the horizon.

He said: 'Mr Jexon, if you really are the person responsible for bringing me here, then you have a lot to explain.'

The man said: 'It's Doctor Jexon.'

'I'm sorry.'

'We have similar interests, Doctor Wentik. We're both scientists. I'm a sociologist. I deal with the abstract concepts of people, government and movement. On the other hand you, I believe, are a research biochemist, treating with compounds and chemicals. As such, we are both professional rationalists.'

'I'll go along with that,' Wentik said, cautiously.

'In which case, your rationalism should tell you that before I can explain to you, I must know what it is that requires the explanation.'

'You mean you don't know what's been happening to me for the last twelve weeks ?'

'No. All I know is that something which should have taken only a matter of days to accomplish has only now been completed. That is, my meeting you.'

'Have you no idea what has delayed it?'

'None whatsoever.'

So Wentik told him what had happened.

There, in the tiny green craft, travelling slowly and without apparent source of power across a city totally alien to him, Wentik recounted the entire sequence of events. He started from the time Astourde and Musgrove had come to him at the Concentration – at the mention of Astourde's name, Jexon questioned Wentik sharply – told about the episode at the jail, and then about his being taken to the hospital. The only detail he consciously omitted was the previous night's sexual innovation.

When he'd finished, Jexon said: 'You say that this man Astourde has died?'

'It was an accidental death. He spilled some aviation spirit and ignited it before he could get away.'

'And there were other men with you? Have you any idea who they were?'

'No. As far as I could make out they were in the American army at some time, but that wasn't very clear.'

'Where are they now?'

'I assume they're still at the jail,' Wentik replied. 'They've got a helicopter with them, and one of the men can fly it. They might have moved by now.'

'Can you tell me anything else about Astourde?'

'Not really. All I know is that he worked for a government department, and that he was supposed to be investigating the Planalto District for them.'

'I'm intrigued with what you say about this interrogation,' Jexon said. 'Have you any idea of his motivations?'

Wentik thought for a moment.

'Again, I'm not certain. I think he became confused; one of the other men implied as much when he said something about

Astourde "blaming" me for everyone being at the jail. He had told the other men that I had brought them, for example. But as far as I was concerned, it was clear who brought who.'

'I think I can solve that for you,' Jexon said.

He tightened his grip on the controls, and the nose of the aircraft dipped. At once the rush of air past it increased, and Wentik felt the machine swoop down positively towards the ground.

In front of them he now saw a large building spreading across several acres of ground. Although he had difficulty telling an old building from a new one here, this one appeared to have the weathering of several years on its concrete fascia. The plane circled round it, then descended silently towards a small lawn where several similar machines were parked. When the machine was still, Jexon stood up.

Wentik said: 'Aren't you going to tell me how this thing works?'

'Later,' Jexon laughed. 'It's our one big contribution to the world, and we don't just drop it casually into conversation. I'll tell you this afternoon, along with anything else you may want to know. But first I've got to make a couple of calls. I didn't know that there was anyone else involved.'

'But you knew about Musgrove.'

'Oh yes. He is the central character, in fact.'

The man strode away, and Wentik hurried after him into the building.

Jexon rejoined Wentik early in the afternoon. Wentik had spent the morning in his new apartment and the laboratory attached to it.

As Jexon had implied, it was a part of the University. Wentik had a complete apartment set aside for him, containing every comfort he could imagine, including, to his private amusement, a television set. But he was far more interested in the laboratory which, Jexon told him before leaving him, was for his exclusive use. There was as much assistance as he wanted, both student and qualified, and all he needed to do was ask. He examined the lab carefully, and found in it virtually every piece of equipment he had been using at the Concentration.

Around noon, a student brought him some food and gave him a complete new wardrobe of clothes – far more than he could ever conceive of needing. He took them politely, and put them in one of the several closets around the apartment. Later, he changed his clothes, and put on a fresh pair of the trousers and shirt.

At two o'clock Jexon came in.

Wentik was relaxing in one of the well-padded easy-chairs, enjoying the luxury of the air-conditioning. Outside, the heat was at its daytime high, and there was an atmosphere of tired enervation smothering the city.

Jexon went to a cabinet and poured two long drinks, liberally laced with ice and fruit-peel. He passed one to Wentik.

'I've just been to see Musgrove,' he said. 'He's in the hospital, having the treatment they were trying to give you.'

'He's fortunate,' said Wentik, thinking of the hours he'd spent with Karena the night before. Did Musgrove qualify for such treatment? he wondered.

'Again, I can only apologize for that. Like most of the other things, that was my fault I'm afraid. I'd arranged for you to be met at the airport, and for Musgrove to be taken to hospital. When the plane landed the ambulance crew was there, but my man wasn't. Because you were in the strait-jacket, they mistook you for Musgrove.'

'Why didn't you look for me at the hospital?'

'We had no reason to suppose you were there. Musgrove ran off soon after you had left – he told me this morning he was trying to escape – and I assumed that you were somewhere in the city and that Musgrove was in hospital. The truth, in fact, was of course the other way round. Anyhow, it's sorted out now.'

Wentik sipped at his glass, and found the drink was delicious: a sweet, refreshing punch with an unidentifiable spice about it.

'I really didn't mind,' he said, thinking of Karena again. 'It gave me a very welcome rest. How did you find Musgrove in the end?'

'As soon as we discovered he was in the city somewhere, we put out a call and he turned up in less than fifteen minutes. A police-squad had been holding him for about thirty-six hours.'

Wentik frowned slightly at the implicit enigma in this remark.

He wondered at a police unit holding a man without referring it to higher authority, but let it go. There was probably some explanation somewhere.

'Anyway,' Jexon continued. 'That's no longer the problem. The fact is that you're here.'

Wentik said: 'Which, I suppose, brings us back to my question: *Why* am I here?'

Jexon smiled. 'To do a job. Perhaps not a very easy one or a very pleasant one, but nevertheless a job for which you are the only person qualified.'

'And that is?'

'To put right what you've done, Doctor Wentik. To help us put together human society. To correct a wrong. Call it anything you like, but it's got to be done.'

'*What* has to be done?' Wentik said softly.

'The disturbance gas must be disposed of.' Jexon took a long draught from his glass, then watched Wentik for reaction.

Wentik shrugged.

'Is this what Astourde was talking about? He said the reason I was here was because of my work.'

'Exactly. You created the disturbance gas ... you must now destroy it.'

'And if I don't? Or can't?'

'You'll have to. I can give you very good reasons why you should. And anyway, when you can appreciate for yourself the damaging effects it has on our society, then I'm sure you will do what is necessary. If you don't ... Well, that is up to you. You can tell us what you wish, and our own scientists and technologists will have to tackle it by themselves.'

Wentik said: 'I'm not inhuman, Jexon, but after what I've been through you would have to give me very good reasons why I should do anything at all for you.'

'I think I can supply those. But you should remember one thing before you make up your mind: there can be no going back to your own time. Your world is dead, and has been for over two hundred years.'

Wentik watched him without expression.

'I think I can comprehend that,' he said slowly.

'You accept, then, the nature of what we have done to you? That we have brought off a kind of transfer through time to bring you here?'

'Yes.'

'I congratulate you.'

'Doctor Jexon,' Wentik said. 'Perhaps we could get back to the main point. You were going to explain why I should work on this disturbance gas for you.'

'All right,' Jexon said. He drained his glass, and went to the cabinet for another.

'I see that you have read our doctrinaire history,' he said, indicating the slim volume that lay on the table between them. 'In that you will have read of the war that took place in 1989. That was a dreadful war; a total and final war. In a matter of weeks nearly ninety per cent of the world's population was either killed or fatally infected. Out of the debris of that holocaust, we have rebuilt.

'The war has left its legacy. Not only have whole nations been destroyed, cities razed and entire races wiped out, but there are side-effects which even today, two hundred years afterwards, still bring chaos to our world.

'There is radiation. We have no way of telling how many nuclear weapons were exploded, or how much radiation was released. But we know the residual effects of it, and if you were to come with me to some areas of the globe you would be able to see with your own eyes. Remember America? Remember the richest, most powerful nation on Earth? No one lives there now. It's got the highest radiation-count in the world. One day we'll probably try to recolonize it, but not yet.

'Then there are the germs and microbes. Fortunately their effects were short-lived and we run no risk from them now. But I can take you down to the botanical museum and show you corn-husks four feet long, and simple fruits like apples and bananas that grow on ordinary trees, yet which would poison any man who ate them. And I could show photographs of the deformed children that have been born. I could provide you with evidence of cancer-viruses, and all manner of by-products from the bacteria thrown into the atmosphere during the war. What the germs themselves can no longer do to us, the product of two hundred years of cross-pollination and background radiation is doing to the products of the products of these original germs.

'But radiation and bacteria we can grow to live with. Every year that passes reduces their potency, and all we need to eventually conquer them is patience.

'Disturbances we cannot live with, because they have not lost their potency with the passage of time.

'In the closing stages of the war the opposing powers grew desperate. As the bombing continued and still each enemy fought back, different kinds of weapons were used, many of them untried. Among these was what we now call the disturbance gas. The chemical composition of this we still do not properly know. But one of the powers, and we have reason to believe it was the United States, released thousands of tons of this gas into the atmospheres of their opponents. If the gas had behaved like every other gas, it would have done its job and then dispersed. But this one didn't. There was something about its composition that its users could not have foreseen. Instead of dispersing, the gas aggregated and retained much of its potency. The clouds of it started moving through the atmosphere, at the will of the prevailing winds.'

Wentik said: 'I read in the book of the Disturbances. What were those?'

'They were what happened when human beings breathed the gas.

'There would be a community going about its everyday existence in whichever way it chose. Perhaps things were uncivilized then, but what else could be expected? There were almost no communications. Slowly, things would begin to degenerate. A fight here, a rape there, someone becoming physically ill somewhere else. In about three days the whole community would be affected by it, and, depending on the normal state of affairs there, one of several things would happen. People living from hand to mouth would band together and kill the weakest members of their community; a religiously oriented, group would go into a near-frenzy of worship;

a militant society would form bands of self-styled vigilantes and go on a murderous, and often suicidal, rampage against their neighbours. It varied in every case, but the outcome was always pretty much the same: a Disturbance. It was worse in the big cities, and less serious in direct proportion to the number of people involved.

'This went on probably from the end of the war in 1990 until about 2085 or 2090. Only in the last thirty years of this did it have its label.

'During the nineties, the Disturbances suddenly abated, and it is from this time that the Reformation begins. The cities were repopulated and rebuilt, we developed our technology, and built a society which some people of your time might have thought to be nearly perfect.

'But the Disturbances had not finished. For some reason which we do not know, the disturbance gas had changed its activity. Now instead of being blown around the world at will, it collected at an approximate altitude of three thousand feet above sea-level, and stayed there. To our knowledge it still moves around the world, but as far as we here in Brazil are concerned, only those parts of the country in the mountains or on the plateaus are affected.'

Wentik said: 'Areas such as the Planalto District, I presume.'

'Yes,' Jexon said.

'Ordinarily, this wouldn't bother us,' he went on, 'because a major part of Brazil's economy has always been based upon its coastal region. But because we have an expanding population and the high parts of Brazil contain the largest mineral deposits in the world we need to be able to work in those regions. Not only this, but we still feel the effects of the disturbance gas down here. About three or four times a year, usually in spring or autumn, a storm blows up inland and some of the gas is blown down here.'

Jexon raised his glass in an ironic toast.

'And that, Doctor Wentik, is what we want you to do for us. You invented the gas, you must destroy it.'

Eighteen

•

Wentik finished his own drink, and refilled his glass. Meanwhile, he thought about what Jexon had told him.

His major problem was an acceptance that it had in fact been his work that created the disturbance gas. What Astourde had said earlier had been substantially the same, yet hadn't carried conviction.

He said: 'How do you connect me with this?'

'We found some old records when Washington was searched. Anything that survived the war was brought to São Paulo for examination, and in due course of time we found a reference to your work.'

'But my work was concerned with mental conditioning. Not warfare.'

Jexon said: 'To most Brazilians it's the same thing.'

'Not at all. The way this disturbance gas was used, or at least the way you described it to me, it seems likely it was devised expressly as an anti-civilian personnel weapon.'

'Isn't that what any kind of conditioning is?'

'Perhaps.'

Wentik sat in thought for a while. He remembered reading the theories of Pavlov, then discovering how they'd been applied in practice by Josef Stalin in the Soviet Union. It was all part of the permanent gulf between theory and practice, between the cold clinical light of a research-bench and the blinding heat of an interrogation-room. A scientist may develop a principle and produce something which is eventually, used to ends totally abhorrent to the original scientist. Pavlov was no tyrant of doctrinaire science, though his methods had been used in such a way.

And now Wentik was having to face the possibility that the same had happened to him.

Jexon said: 'Couldn't you tell me what your work was intended to do?'

'I thought you knew.'

'You seem doubtful that your work and our Disturbances can be connected. If you tell me exactly what it was you were doing, I'll describe the psychological process that takes place on a subject, and perhaps you'll see my meaning.'

'All right.'

Wentik found himself beginning to relax. The other man's incisive manner acted as a direct complement to his own rather negative feelings.

As briefly as possible he described his attempts to short-cut Pavlov, and the various processes he had used. He told Jexon about the rats, and how his work had been temporarily held up at the time he was taken to Brazil.

'Did you administer the substance to any men?' Jexon said.

Wentik shook his head.

'I did take some very mild dosages myself, but wouldn't allow it to be tested on anyone else. At the strengths I was using, it had very little effect.'

'And . . . ?'

'And nothing. That's as far as it got.'

'I don't understand.'

'You should. That was when friends Astourde and Musgrove appeared. I had to abandon the work and go with them. As far as I know, that's the situation now.'

Jexon said: 'I assure you it isn't. The information we have in our archives is that your work was completed and the compound developed into a gas we now call the disturbance gas.'

'Your information's wrong. I never finished.'

Jexon shrugged.

'Let me tell you the effects of the gas, in detail,' he said.' The first symptom is always a marked increase in the incidence and vividness of dreams. Then headaches or migraine appear.

'From here, symptoms tend to vary from one individual to another. The one thing common to all is a subtle emphasis of character. Suppose one is by nature a little irascible, then one's tendency to become irritated or bad-tempered is increased. Another person of a retiring nature, say, would become progressively negative, and would shrink from contact.

'All this happens if there is no external stimulus. In practice, of course, humans are inherently gregarious and interact with one another. One person alone might never realize the psychological changes taking place inside him. Even two people might get along for weeks without any basic change taking place, if the two were part of a sound and compatible relationship. But any number more than this, and a general decline into mania soon follows.'

Wentik said: 'I think I can see why. If, as you say, this disturbance gas is my compound, then this could be accounted for quite logically. The substance opens the mind to a new belief which, without conscious stimulus, is never there. The process to this point is the equivalent of Pavlov's shock-techniques, but in a chemical or metabolic sense. Without the stimulus, the unconscious turns to itself for stimulation and exaggerates itself. But if there is interaction between people, there is a constant bombardment of unintentional stimuli, and an irrational pattern of behaviour takes over.'

Jexon nodded his agreement.

'You've arrived in ten seconds at the conclusion it took us nearly as many years to reach. But then, we expected you to. Doesn't that convince you, as it does me, that this is your substance? '

Wentik said: 'I'm afraid it does.'

'I saw Musgrove this morning,' Jexon said after a while, 'and I can put together a rough picture of what happened when you first arrived in Brazil.'

'You mean at the jail?'

Jexon nodded. 'It's not too clear; Musgrove is very confused about a lot of it. But he's helped me make some sense out of what you told me, and I've patched together the rest.

'But first, you were curious about the way our machines are

powered. That is called *Poder Directo,* or Direct Power in English. This, as I implied this morning, is Brazil's major contribution to technology. In its simplest form it could be described as transmitted electricity, but in practice I'm told it is a lot more complicated. I don't understand these things myself. All you need to know about it is that under certain stress-patterns, electric current takes on a form that can be radiated, rather like radio waves. This makes power enormously flexible, and much more convenient. There is virtually no limit to the number of devices that can be run off it at any one time, provided they are within range of the transmitter.

'The discovery of Direct Power was, like most significant scientific advances, unexpected and accidental. And it opened up several new lines of research. One of those led to the development of the displacement-field.'

Wentik said: 'You're going too fast. Is Direct Power what propels your aircraft?'

'Yes. And everything in this apartment, and at the hospital. And at the jail.'

'Then why was the VTOL that picked me up equipped with ordinary turbines?'

'Because Direct Power must be transmitted. Anything that moves outside the effective field must take its own power with it.'

'Go on.'

'I was saying that this led to the discovery of the displacement-field. You would call it time-travel, I suppose, but it's not as facile as that. The field that is generated disrupts part of the temporal field that exists in balance with normal space. Again, the mathematics of this are slightly beyond me ... but the effect is simple enough. The transmitter, and anyone or anything within its range, is moved through time. The amount of travel is not determinable, or at least it isn't at the moment. The span covered by the generator is a little under two hundred years, though I'm told that there is occasional slight distortion.

'Elapsed subjective time, therefore, is the same. A man can travel into the past from here, and emerge during the latter half of 1989. He may spend six months there, and on return find six months have elapsed here.'

'How did I become involved in this?' Wentik said, more to himself than to the other man. A mood of melancholy had settled on him. Perhaps it was the drink.

Jexon looked at him, and for a moment Wentik thought he detected a glimpse of sympathy in the man's expression.

'It happened,' he said,' that at about the same time as the first experiments with the displacement-field were being conducted, we came across the reference to your work. It was suggested at the time that someone return in time to ask you to come and sort out the damage you had inadvertently caused, but it took several years for the progress of elapsed time to bring us to a date two hundred years after a time we could trace you. As soon as we knew where you were – the only records we had said that you went to work for the Genex Chemical Corporation in October 1988 – we sent a man back to get you. That man was Musgrove.'

Wentik looked up sharply.

'Musgrove works for you? I thought he was something to do with Astourde.'

'No, he's been one of my assistants here for years. He's done a lot of background work on the effects of the disturbance gas on our society, and I thought he would be the ideal man for the task.'

Wentik said: 'But he never told me this.'

'No . .. There were several factors that I didn't take into account. The first was the extreme effect the disturbance gas had on him, and the second was his meeting Astourde.

'Musgrove left São Paulo about ten months ago. His brief was simple: to go back to 1988 by use of the displacement-field, approach you and explain what had happened, and bring you back here with him. You would then have the option, when you had completed your work, of staying here or returning to your own time. It was our hope and belief that you would stay, when you had what was to be your immediate future – in other words, the impending war – revealed to you.

'However, things began to go wrong.

'Musgrove was flown to the jail in the Planalto District with a displacement-field generator. The transfer had to be done from there because the generator will only work in regions where there is little surface undulation and a minimum of trees and shrubbery. Also, for obvious social reasons, the area must be unpopulated. Areas like that are rare enough in Brazil, as I think you can imagine.

'The field-generator, which in this case was also able to double as a Direct Power transmitter, was installed according to plan, and the pilot of the VTOL returned to São Paulo.

'During this time Musgrove must have become accidentally exposed to the disturbance gas. As you have observed, it is particularly dense in the Planalto District. From this point, his actions began to take on a pattern of randomness. He must have used the displacement-field correctly, and returned the jail and its environs to 1988. His instructions from here were that he should go to the Genex Corporation in Minneapolis. Instead, he went to Washington, where he turned up some months later. What happened to him in the intervening period I do not know. This morning when I talked to him he was very confused about it. I can only assume that he wandered for some time in the jungle before encountering an outpost of civilization, from where he proceeded to America.

'In Washington, he met Astourde.

'Now you'll have to try to imagine what these two men were like at the time they met. Musgrove is a normally stable man, but the effects of the disturbance gas can last for weeks. For a considerable period he had been alone in jungle surroundings of extreme unpleasantness. It is fair to assume that when he met Astourde, he was suffering from acute schizophrenia.

'Astourde, on the other hand, sounds from your description as if he suffered from paranoia. He was physically unprepossessing, held down an unattractive job in Washington, and was probably unpopular with his colleagues. His marriage was breaking up. Such a person often suffers from the delusions that are the roots of paranoid behaviour, and Astourde could have been no exception.

'Already he had been involved with the American government's investigation of our displacement-field, squatting rudely in the middle of the Brazilian jungle, and Musgrove had inevitably been brought into contact with him.

'Astourde was his pompous and overbearing self and poor

Musgrove, still suffering from the effects of the disturbance gas, fell sharply under his influence.

'From then on, it was Astourde's show.'

Wentik said: 'When I first met them, I was impressed with Musgrove, but Astourde dominated. I suppose this was why.'

'The next part of the story you are familiar with,' Jexon said. 'Astourde had pulled strings and organized himself what amounted to a private army. In taking you to the jail he felt he could investigate the phenomena he'd been commissioned to explain, and at the same time Musgrove's mission, as it had been scantily explained to him, would be fulfilled.

'Then a third unforeseen factor presented itself. That is, the effect of the disturbance gas on Astourde and the other men.

'Astourde felt he had some power over you; the disturbance syndrome translated this to a certainty and an interrogation was commenced. The men felt themselves to be under Astourde's command, and became his virtual slaves. Astourde, convinced that you were in some way behind everything, blamed you for the new predicament and tried to stir up feeling against you in the men. Musgrove, hopelessly confused, retreated to the cells.

'In the middle of all this, you retained your sanity and reason yet, disoriented by what was happening, could only observe.'

Wentik said: 'Astourde was aware that everyone except me was experiencing what he called violent fantasies.'

'You appear to be immune to the disturbance gas. Have you any idea why?'

'Not really,' Wentik said. 'Only that the quantities I took at the Concentration may have hardened my resistance to it. Do you find immunity to it here in people exposed to the gas more than once?'

Jexon shook his head. 'There's no record of it. If it were some protection we would find a way of using it.'

'I was injecting myself,' Wentik pointed out. 'Were you?'

'It might make a difference,' Wentik said.

'Could you reproduce the substance here in the laboratory?'

'I expect so. It takes time, though.'

'No matter,' Jexon said. 'Anyway, for reasons I cannot determine,

Musgrove suddenly left the jail on foot and did what he was supposed to do in the first place: radio for help. Surrounding the jail are several unmanned guard-boxes, and each has a short-wave kit. An aircraft was sent to pick him up, and four days ago he arrived back here in São Paulo. Without you.'

'Four days ago I was still at the jail.'

'Of course. I didn't realize Musgrove's condition, and when he said that he had brought you as far as the jail and that you were still there, I sent him back at once. Remember, I had been waiting ten months without news or explanation. Fortunately, the two crew-members of the aircraft must have realized what was going on when they arrived at the jail, and put Musgrove into a strait-jacket as well as you. It's our standard procedure for people afflicted with the Disturbance.'

'There's one thing I'm still not sure I understand,' Wentik said. 'And that's the jail. What is it doing up there, if the disturbance gas is known to have such a profound effect on people?'

'Another legacy from the past,' Jexon replied. 'Several years ago, scientists were tackling the problem of clearing the Amazon basin. Nothing can be done there while the jungle covers everything. The terrain is so difficult to work in that it is virtually impossible to clear it by conventional methods. So they devised unconventional ones. Nowadays, the work of clearing the jungle in the Manaus region is done by aerial spray-processes. The trees, of such a diversity of type that they could never be industrially exploited, are poisoned from the air and left to rot. In less than six months they reach a state of decay from which they can be pulped on the spot, and either used as cheap industrial fuel or as soil-humus in the areas of the country endowed with less fertile ground.

'These processes were pioneered in the part of the jungle we now call the Planalto District. Every now and then we fly over and respray it, to keep the stubble down.

'But about a hundred years ago, while the Disturbances were at their height and their causes were not fully known, a new prison was needed, and the Planalto District seemed to be an ideal place for it. Remote and virtually escape-proof, it was considered at the time to represent the peak of the technique of applied corrective therapy. Nowadays, we know more about the effects of the disturbance gas, and the jail has been closed for years.'

Wentik sat in silence, remembering the empty cells and corridors, and the locked doors.

Jexon said: 'Is there anything else you want to know?'

Wentik thought for a moment. Then he said: 'What happened to the men who wandered accidentally into the Planalto District? Astourde told me that several had disappeared, and he had taken a photograph of your aircraft when it was picking up one of them. And what about Astourde's men who are still at the jail?'

'They'll be picked up tomorrow. We make regular flights through the regions affected by the disturbance gas. People wander in from time to time, and have difficulty in getting out again. The Planalto District, because it has been cleared, is one of the regions we patrol regularly. If men from your time had wandered in, then they'd be taken to hospital and given rehabilitation treatment.'

He stopped, took a pen from his pocket, and scribbled something down on to a sheet of paper.

'I'll look into this as well. It's probable they are still in hospital, because it would appear to the doctors that they are stubborn cases. They would maintain their stories, and the doctors would be thinking that they are clinging to their delusions.'

Suddenly his face became grim.

'This business is beginning to have serious consequences,' he said.

'But what will happen to them now?' Wentik said, realizing the cause for Jexon's seriousness. The men were accidental victims of the process of events, and would be deeply affected by what had been happening to them.

Jexon looked round helplessly. 'I suppose they'll have to be offered the same alternatives as you. Stay here and work for the good of the community, or be returned to their own time.'

'I think I can speak for them,' Wentik said. 'Even though I know none of them. They'll want to be returned.'

Jexon shook his head. 'I doubt it. Do you know what the date is?'

'Mine or yours?'

'The one you've been subconsciously oriented to all the time you've been here. 1989.'

'Sometime in August, I imagine.'

'It's the 5th August.'

'That's significant?'

'Not in itself. But they're fighting a war at the moment. You remember reading about the Cuban invasion of Florida? That was on 14th July 1989. The fighting was finished on 22nd July. On the 28th, Havana was reprisal-bombed. On the 29th another Cuban city, Manzanillo, was destroyed.

'Yesterday, Doctor Wentik, as you lay in that hospital room, the American President rejected the demands of the Soviet Praesidium. Russia had demanded immediate patriation of all Cuban citizens in a neutral zone on the American mainland plus an unequivocal assurance of progress to socialist rule in the United States within a decade.

'Today, even as we are sitting here in this comfortable room, men in your time are taking the first steps towards mutual destruction. The Russian fleet in the Mediterranean will be destroyed this afternoon. By evening, the first nuclear weapons will be exploding on American soil.'

Wentik said: 'There's no doubt of this?'

'None whatsoever.'

The man got to his feet, and put on his green cape.

'I'd better get to the hospital and see about those other men. In the meantime, you might like to read this.'

He took a slim booklet, similar to the history, from a pocket and passed it to Wentik.

'It's one of my own books, and it might help you acclimatize to our society a little quicker.'

Wentik took it, and placed it absently on the table next to the other one. As the man reached the door, he called after him.

'Doctor Jexon!'

'Yes?*

'I wonder if you could do me a small favour at the hospital? There is a nurse . . .'

The man smiled.

'Don't tell me. I'll put the word round. She'll find you.' And he went out. Wentik sat down again, and pulled the book towards him.

Nineteen

•

There are two obsessions common to all men, present in varying proportions. One is the quest for love, and the other for truth.

There is no substitute for either of these, though love may be temporarily supplanted by the physical process of sex. There is no quieting truth.

Wentik lay awake, his right arm around the shoulders of the sleeping girl next to him. The night was warm, and although it was the early hours of the morning, the city throbbed around him. There were no quiet hours in São Paulo, the entire population geared to a voluntary shift-pattern that allowed for the functioning of the city to continue for twenty-four hours a day.

In the dark, Wentik stared at the ceiling, overpowering images of the early years of his marriage threatening to overcome him. For the first time since his enforced separation from Jean had begun, he relaxed in a comforting pool of sentiment. The memory of her physical features – wide forehead, freckled forearms, small soft breasts, rapid laugh – came poignantly to him from across the months. These are the objects of memory; not major or important subtleties of character, but superficialities whose presence, associated with recalled incidents, make up a remembered identity. His life with Jean had been pleasant; he could describe it no better. She meant a lot to him, and they had known a kind of happiness that could not be described to others: they were content, and perhaps complacent. But no one minded. If love was what he had shared with her, then his lust for Karena had temporarily diminished it.

But it returned.

In the same way, what Jexon had told him that afternoon had temporarily stilled his questioning of what was happening to him. But now, given the peace of solitude he saw one great absence of truth.

The disturbance gas, the mysterious substance he had been brought here to destroy, could not be his.

The work he had been doing, true enough, would lead eventually to a substance whose effect on a human brain would be similar to that described by Jexon.

But he hadn't finished.

Astourde and Musgrove had interrupted him, taken him away from his work before he had reached its conclusion.

The girl in his arms turned in her sleep, and rested her head more firmly in the pit of his arm. He held her tightly, his hand falling across her chest and gently cupping one of her breasts.

Then who . . . ? Who was it who had continued his work in his absence? Only N'Goko had his papers.

Wentik sat up sharply. *Abu N'Goko.*

Impatient with the slowness of the research progress, impatient to try the substance on human volunteers, impatient . . . He said aloud: 'N'Goko!'

And the girl fell back on to the pillows, frowning in the dark at the disturbance.

PART THREE

The Concentration

Twenty

•

Three thousand feet beneath them, the jungle spread to both horizons. Wentik sat with Jexon in the cabin of the VTOL, a dozen strait-jackets hanging ominously on a rack behind them.

Wentik was feeling apprehensive about what they would find at the jail. Only when they had set out had he realized the growing unease he felt about Astourde's death. If one man could die like that, then it was possible that more could. The men had many weapons at the jail, including rifles and knives, though what Astourde's motives in bringing them with him had been, Wentik could not understand. If the men got it into their heads that the rifles had been brought for the purpose of fighting …

He glanced across at the old man sitting next to him, his back straight and his head held proudly. It was as if he were refusing to admit even to himself the gradual grip that old age was tightening around him. Wentik had read the man's book, written within the last two years, and had been impressed with the vivid clarity of his style, the precision of his vocabulary.

Jexon suddenly touched his arm, and pointed down through the port.

'See, we're just coming into the cleared region.'

Beneath them, the jungle was slowly thinning out to the untidy scrubland that Wentik had observed before at the perimeter of the Planalto District. He looked forward, but the usual haze of this region prevented him from seeing clearly what was ahead.

Jexon said: 'Time for the masks, I think.'

He reached behind him, and pulled forward the portable oxygen apparatus. Provided that a man avoided breathing the polluted air, he could move with complete freedom and lack of other protection in the affected areas.

Wentik said: 'I don't think I'll bother with the mask. I've survived here before.'

'It's up to you,' Jexon replied. 'But I wouldn't walk around without one.'

'You're not immune.'

'No. But then you don't know how long you will be.'

'I'll be all right.'

Part of the truth of it was that Wentik disliked the feel of the rubber mask on his face. However rationally he tried to view it, his proneness to his own peculiar brand of claustrophobia manifested itself whenever his normal breathing was interrupted in any way, even though the masks Jexon used covered only the nose, leaving the mouth free to speak. To this extent, his feeling of immunity from the gas was only an excuse. But in addition he really did feel instinctively that his immunity was permanent.

In the cockpit, the two pilots slipped into their own masks, and switched on the oxygen supply. Wentik reflected how seriously these people took the effects of the gas, and he wondered what fate would befall him if it were made public in São Paulo that he was partially responsible for its creation.

Less than two minutes later the aircraft was over the jail, and began a wide slow circling of the building. All four men on board began searching the ground below for some sight of Astourde's men, but they were nowhere in view.

The black scar where the burned remains of the maze-shack disfigured the uniform green-brown of the stubble brought a sharp, unpleasant recollection to Wentik of Astourde's death, and he looked away quickly.

'What do you think?' he said to Jexon. 'Are they inside the jail, or would they have been more likely to move away?'

'Who can tell? 'His voice was slightly nasal and muffled because of the mask.' There would be no pattern to their movements.'

He leaned forward and touched the pilot's shoulder.

'Hover outside the front of the building. If they're inside they'll come out to investigate.'

The man nodded, and swung the craft across the building to where the helicopter was still parked. At least, thought Wentik, they haven't flown that anywhere.

The pilot brought the craft down to about fifty feet, and held it stationary. The hover-jets in the belly of the machine settled into a grinding roar that shook the whole aircraft and must have made a deafening noise that could be heard anywhere in the jail. Jexon and Wentik watched the main gate.

After about five minutes it opened, and the men appeared.

They came out together, looking up at the aircraft warily.

None of them was carrying any kind of weapon. They walked until they were about twenty-five yards from the piece of ground over which the aircraft was hovering, and stopped.

Jexon said to the pilot: 'Can you get them from here?'

The man said: 'Leave it to me.'

Curious to see what would happen, Wentik watched the men on the ground. Without warning, a cloud of yellow vapour was emitted from the side of the aircraft and bellowed outwards and down. Part of it was caught in the mighty downdraught from the engines and whipped outwards from the aircraft and around the men. One or two tried to back away, but in seconds the whole group was surrounded in the vapour and lost to sight.

'Take her down,' Jexon said to the pilot, and Wentik felt that drooping sensation as the nose lowered. Unlike a helicopter, which lands in a slightly nose-up attitude, the VTOL adopted a forward-sloping angle.

As the plane settled on the stubble, the blast from the jets blew away the remainder of the vapour, and Wentik saw the men lying unconscious.

Jexon said: 'It's almost instantaneous in its action, but really very mild. When they wake up they won't even have a headache.'

Wentik recalled that after his experience of the vapour, he'd been able to consume a bowl of spicy soup almost immediately.

As soon as the engines had stilled, all four men in the plane stood up, and went down to the hatch. The pilot opened it, and they stepped out on to the stubble.

Wentik looked across at the jail, a black shape blocking out the sun. It was just a building; any attributes of menace he felt for it came from his own subconscious, not from anything about the architecture.

Jexon said to him: 'Are all the men here?'

Wentik looked down at them. Counting heads, he thought. There were twelve.

'Yes,' he said.

'Good.' Jexon nodded to the pilot and the other man, who bent down and gently lifted the first unconscious man towards the aircraft.

'Leave that to them. Can you take me to the cell with the Direct Power transmitter?'

Wentik nodded, and led the man through the main gate, along the narrow tunnel, and up the flight of stairs to the first floor of the jail.

As they walked along the corridor, passing the cell which Wentik had first used, he said: 'Have you been to the jail before?'

'Once. Several years ago, shortly after it was closed down.' He looked round at the cells they were passing.' I can understand Musgrove becoming infected, now I'm here. Everything feels absolutely normal. One is tempted to take off the mask.'

Wentik said: 'It depends on viewpoint, I suppose. I find the atmosphere of the jail frightening.'

'I can't see why.'

'You've never been here as a prisoner.'

The man said nothing to this, and they walked on. When they reached the narrow staircase leading up to Astourde's old office Wentik led the way again. His impulse was to take the steps two at a time, but the other man, weighed down both by the cylinders and his years, took the climb more steadily.

As they walked along the second corridor towards the cell containing the machine, Wentik asked: 'When I've found N'Goko, where are you going to pick me up?'

'Here at the jail.'

'But how will I get back into the Planalto District?'

'I'll explain that in a moment. You've got the currency I gave you. Spend as much of it as you have to in getting N'Goko back. I probably won't be here myself, but I'll make sure one of the aircraft will be.'

Wentik nodded, then winced slightly as a jab of pain pierced his temples.

Jexon had said: '– headaches or migraine appear –' He shook his head quickly. It was the oppressive sensation the jail induced in him. Nothing more.

They came to the cell, and Jexon pushed the door open, straining as the base of it grated against the concrete floor. He reached in, switched on the light, and the two men walked in.

Jexon was bending over the switch at the back of the machine that was set in the three-way channel.

'This is it,' he said. 'The crux of the whole operation, here in one lever.'

Wentik said: 'I was looking at that. What does it do?'

'It controls the type of field that is generated. I can't tell you how the machine works, though it was explained to me once. That's not my concern ... I'm more interested in what it does. In essence, the generator has four states: three types of *on,* as it were, and one type of *off.* It's at *off* at the moment.'

Wentik saw that the tiny switch was at the neutral position of the three-pointed star, exactly as he had found it before, and as he had left it.

Jexon explained: 'In its present position it is truly off. That is to say, the machine is generating no kind of field at all.

'If I push it upwards' – he did so, and next to it the panel marked 'AA' came alight – 'the field is switched on. If we were to walk out to the edge of the field, we could see the jungle that exists in your time, 1989. We could step into it, and back again. In other words, there is a true pocket of our present-time existing in yours.

'When Musgrove was sent back to fetch you he put the field into this condition.'

'But it wasn't like that when I came here. As Musgrove and I stepped across the line I looked back. The jungle had vanished.'

Jexon nodded his agreement. 'That's a safety-device built into the machine. You see, if the field were left in its two-way state, imagine the trouble that could be caused here by people wandering into it. If it were left in its " AA" state, anyone wandering into the field would see exactly the converse of what you did. They'd be walking across the stubble, then they'd turn round and find impenetrable jungle behind them. They step off to investigate, and they're back into your present!'

Wentik said: 'I think I see.'

'So when the field is left generating for more than a determinable time – adjusted on that scale down there,' Jexon pointed to one of the dials on the left, '– it automatically switches down here, to state "AA".'

He moved the lever down, and to the right. The appropriate panel lit up.

'Now, the field allows transit in one direction only. That is, from your present to ours. As far as we here are concerned this is fine. To all intents and purposes nothing has been changed. Once here in *our* present we can walk into and out of the field at will. But from the point of view of a person in 1989, things are a little different.

'There is this inexplicable six-mile circle of stubble in the middle of the Brazilian jungle. We didn't think this would matter, as we didn't anticipate there would be much movement around here in your time, but apparently we were wrong. Also, Musgrove wasn't expected to be very long in fetching you, thus considerably reducing the chances of anyone coming across it. As it happened, he was several months, and in that time several people wandered in. Imagine how it must have seemed to them. A circle of stubble in the centre of the forest ... walk into it, and the forest vanishes ... try to walk out again, and nothing happens. There is no communication from one existence to the other.'

'Astourde told me about a man who had gone into the field accidentally, who had returned to the approximate point of entry and written huge warning signs, presumably with the intention of trying to stop anyone else from following him.'

'Have you any idea of his name?' Jexon asked.

Wentik thought for a moment.

'Brandon, I think. Or Brander. I'm not sure.'

'It's probably Brander. A man of great initiative. He was amongst the first to recover, according to the doctor I spoke to yesterday. He accepted what had happened calmly, and has settled down.'

Wentik nodded thoughtfully. One of the innocent victims of the course of events, now beyond the control of any of them.

'The third state,' Jexon went on, 'is what we call the "BB". This is the selective field.'

He moved the switch, and immediately there was the high-pitched whistling noise that Wentik had heard when he had found the machine.

'What's that noise?' he said.

Jexon opened the inspection-plate, and gingerly pulled down the length of cable.

'This,' he said. 'What you can hear is the noise made by the air between the two terminals which is transmitted backwards to your present. The selective field is just that: anything between the two terminals is transmitted.'

'And where does it reappear?'

'Right here in this spot. But two hundred years ago.'

Jexon switched the lever back to its central position.

'So how do we bring it off?' Wentik said.

'I've given the matter some thought,' Jexon replied. 'I think the best way is this: We'll send you back to 1989 by use of the selective field. You'll be transmitted instantaneously, and without loss of consciousness, but there is no guarantee of where you'll be when you emerge in your time. Presumably somewhere in the jungle, but you've got to face that anyway. Is that all right with you?'

Wentik nodded slowly.

'As soon as you're safely back, and we've given you adequate time to get away from the vicinity of the field, we'll switch to position "AA". That means that when you've found N'Goko, all you need to do is bring him straight to the Planalto District and simply walk up to the jail. There'll be a plane here waiting for you.'

Wentik said: 'Couldn't the jet pick me up from the Concentration?'

'No,' Jexon said, shaking his head with a gesture of irritation. 'That would be impracticable. There's too much time spent on this as it is. I've got my work to get on with. You'll have to make it on your own.'

Wentik stared at him for a moment, but said nothing. Was this a clue to Jexon's motivations? That his own work came before anything else?

'OK,' he said finally. 'I understand;'

'But there's one thing that you must adhere to most strictly. And that is you must not be tempted to go to America. Even parts of northern Brazil and Venezuela received direct fall-out contamination in the course of the war. At the time you get back, nuclear devices will be actually exploding in other parts of the world. We want you back to work for us, even if you can't get to the Concentration.'

That's all right, thought Wentik. I've nothing to go back for now anyway ... *Western and Central Europe laid waste in the second wave of bombing ...*

He said to Jexon in a patient voice: 'I go to the Concentration, I find N'Goko, I bring him back here.'

'Good. Now, is there anything else?'

'Only that I have a splitting headache.'

Jexon looked at him sharply. 'How long have you had it?'

'More of less since we got to the jail.'

'It sounds as if you've been exposed to the disturbance gas ... '

'It's not that, I'm sure.'

Jexon looked doubtful. 'I don't know. Remember what happened to Musgrove. You'd better be on your way. Give me your arm.'

Wentik held it out to him, and Jexon took his wrist and squeezed the flesh until his skin lay tightly against his wrist-bone. Then he took the two sharp terminals of the cable, and pressed them on to the skin.

'This will give momentary pain,' he said, and jabbed the two points home. Wentik winced.

He looked up, seeing the man's face half-lit by the cast of the light-bulb on the other side of the machine.

Jexon said: 'Good-bye for the moment, Doctor Wentik.'

And pulled down the switch.

Wentik fell into darkness. Everything around him was pitch black. He thudded on to something hard that knocked the wind out of him, and six inches away an animal that was big and heavy opened its mouth and screamed into his face.

Twenty-one

•

For five hours Wentik crouched awkwardly in almost total darkness on the branch of the tree, not knowing what was going on around him.

The forest was a place of nightmare. The screaming of the animals went on all night, and although he had heard the noise before it was virtually impossible not to feel panic creeping up on him. However much he rationalized it, the image of ferocious and predatory beasts all around him grew stronger. Finally, by an extreme effort of will, he shut his mind to the noise and told himself again and again that the animals were harmless ... and abruptly his fears vanished.

Later, newer fears manifested themselves.

He had no idea how high up in the tree he was. He didn't dare move in the darkness for fear of falling, and could only inch his body into a slightly less uncomfortable position. Although he felt to either side of him he could find no trace of the trunk of the tree, though it was comforting to realize that the branch he was on was thick and could not be far from the bole.

Something both he and Jexon had not considered: that the displacement-field generator was on the second floor of the building, and thus anyone being sent back via the selective field would emerge in mid-air.

Even more worrying to Wentik was what Jexon had said about turning the displacement-field to its state of simultaneous existence in the two presents. If he did, and Wentik was still here, what would happen to him?

And how long did Jexon think it would take him to get out of the vicinity?

Eventually, when Wentik was beginning to think he could cling to the rough surface of the branch no longer, he detected a faint glow coming from in front of him. Slowly it strengthened until he was able to make out shapes of the nearby branches.

As soon as it was light enough, he looked around carefully, realizing to his dismay that from his position on the branch he could not see the ground. The trunk was not far away, less than ten feet, but the surface of the branch was slick with a soft slime that made a firm grip almost impossible.

With the utmost care, Wentik edged his way along the branch until he reached the trunk.

Here the wood was drier and rougher, and several *liane* creepers clung to it. He took hold of one of these experimentally, and found that its hold on the trunk was almost immovable.

He selected another *liane* and shifted his weight from the branch to the trunk. The creepers held and, feeling great relief, he began lowering himself towards the ground.

His arms, long deprived of exercise, were aching in seconds, and he had descended no more than about ten feet before the whole of his upper body was shaking with pain. There was a branch to his right, and he put one of his feet across to it, taking the weight from his arms.

From his new perch he found he could see the ground, perhaps twenty feet below him. He could almost jump ... Sweat was running down his face, and already a minor swarm of insects was hovering around him. Those Brazilian mosquitoes, whose bite Wentik had felt before.

He swung off the branch and continued his descent. Now he could see the ground his movements were less cautious and he grazed his arms in several places. About eight feet from the ground he let go of the creepers, and with an awkward kicking movement of his legs attempted to push himself away from the trunk. Instead, he fell heavily, rolling across the satchel he carried on his back.

He stood up dazedly, and looked around.

The sun had now evidently risen, for the forest was lit with a dull radiance. The animals were quiet again, and invisible. He took the pack from his back, and put it on the floor. Taking out its contents one by one, he made sure that nothing had been lost in the transit across two hundred years.

There was his supply of food, condensed and dried; it occupied little space but would last him weeks if needed. His water, packed in a flat, plastic canteen. A bundle of maps. A *machete.* A compass. A change of clothing. And the money.

Wentik took out the money and looked at it. Here was a small fortune: nearly forty thousand dollars. Jexon had given it to him, telling him that he would need it. Wentik had had distinct misgivings. Supposing, he said, he was asked where he had got it from?

Who will worry? Jexon, replied. There's a war on. No one will care. Priorities change.

Wentik took out the tube of insect-repellent, and smeared it liberally across his face and arms. There was nothing on Earth that could keep the insects away, but it might help. Indeed, when he had the cream on his face, he felt cooler. But the smell was certainly repellent.

He took a mouthful of water from the canteen, and then was ready.

His first consideration must be to get away from the vicinity of the Planalto District. There was no way of telling when Jexon would switch on the field, and Wentik didn't want to be around when he did. He took out his compass, and consulted his map. There was a tiny village about fifteen miles to the north-west of here, and a Roman Catholic mission situated somewhere down on the banks of the Aripuana river. If possible, he wanted to make one or the other of these by nightfall. He had no intention of spending another night in the jungle.

But fifteen miles of this country ... On foot ... ?

He packed away the rest of his things, and set off at once.

By the time he had gone two hundred yards, he knew he could never do it. It was almost impossible to move. The undergrowth was a tangle of dead creepers, live creepers, thorns, broken branches, stunted sprawling bushes – and nowhere was it less than a foot in depth. He used his *machete* constantly, but made little or no impression on the vegetation. The sweat was pouring down his face again, rendering the repellent useless. Already the first tiny pinpricks of blood had appeared on his forehead, and he knew that by noon his face would be swollen and impossibly painful. He pressed on, growing steadily aware that the direction he took was dictated more by chance than by his compass.

Musgrove must have done this ... Musgrove, the man sent back by Jexon to find him, just as he in his turn had been sent back to find N'Goko. Perhaps Jexon had been puzzled why Musgrove's mental condition had deteriorated by the time he reached civilization, but now it was quite clear to Wentik. A few days hacking through this undergrowth would induce mania in almost anyone.

Especially if they had first been exposed to the disturbance gas ...

Wentik felt a new sense of identity with the man. Sent back to do a fairly straightforward job, but at once beset with sheer practical difficulties.

Jexon had said: A person alone might never realize the psychological changes taking place inside him.

Did Musgrove go on alone through this forest, slowly slipping into an insanity he could not recognize, far less understand? He might know about the disturbance gas, but would not be able to diagnose its symptoms in himself.

Then Wentik remembered the headache he'd experienced shortly after returning to the jail. Jexon had said it was the disturbance gas. Was it? Had his immunity to it gone? If so, then would he too, like Musgrove, slip slowly into a mania that would only manifest itself if he came into contact with some kind of influence? Meanwhile knowing nothing of it?

And he thought of his fear of the animals in the night, and how his fear of them had grown until he had *told himself* they were harmless ...

It gave him cause for thought as he moved on slowly and painfully through the jungle. If it were so, then what?

After about three hours, at a point when he was about to stop for food and a rest, Wentik encountered the corpse.

*

It was lying in the bottom of a rough-cut canoe, which had been dragged up on to the overgrown bank of a small river. It might have been dead three days or three weeks: there was no way of telling. White slugs crawled in its open mouth and staring eyes, and the limbs had been stripped of flesh by insects and birds. Only where clothes still hung to the corpse's frame did any form of flesh exist. And here it rotted and putrefied while clouds of insects hovered around. The smell was disgusting.

Wentik's first instinct was to move on, but the sight of the canoe was temping. As far as he knew he was still within the area of the displacement-field, and with every passing minute he was becoming more anxious to move. With the canoe he could cover considerably more distance than he could on foot.

He went over to it, nauseated by the sight of the corpse.

The body was on its back, the right arm crooked up and over so that the skeletal hand now rested behind the head. One leg was drawn up, and the other flopped over the side of the canoe. The bones of the feet had become detached from the ankle, and lay whitely against the dank brown vegetation.

In the bottom of the canoe was a rusty water-canteen, a wooden paddle and a bundle of rotted cloth.

Wentik lifted the end of the canoe, but dropped it hastily as the corpse rolled heavily against the side. Underneath the body was a patch of dark-green slime, teeming with white maggots.

He backed away, shuddering.

For several minutes he stood helplessly some distance from the canoe, wondering what he should do. Like a man who has discovered some loathsome vermin of which he must dispose, he knew he would have to move the corpse, but he couldn't bring himself to do it.

Finally, he took a handkerchief and tied it as tightly as possible over his nose and mouth. Then he found a broken branch in the undergrowth and dragged it over to the canoe.

Averting his gaze, he shoved the end of the branch under the canoe and tried to lever it up. Three times, the end of the branch snapped as soon as he put any pressure against it, and in the end it broke in half across the middle.

Angrily, he threw the end he was holding into the water, went over to the canoe and lifted it bodily. The end came up, the whole thing tipped to the side, and the corpse fell out of it with a horrible loose knocking against the wood, and rolled down the bank into the stream, one of its legs detaching itself and lying half in and half out of the water.

Still shuddering, Wentik watched the corpse settle, until it floated just beneath the surface. The features were so indistinct he could hardly tell, but it seemed to him it was floating face upwards. He stood for a moment and watched it as the sluggish current picked it up, and it began its two-thousand-mile journey towards the sea.

He pushed the canoe down to the edge of the water, and submerged it.

At first the green slime and the maggots maintained their grip on the rough wood, but finally, after repeated sousings, he had the whole craft cleaned out.

He looked around the clearing. Already, the cloud of insects attracted by the corpse had dissipated. Only his own private swarm remained.

When the canoe had been made fast once again on the bank he moved away from it, and sat down on a low branch of a tree some twenty yards back. Here he ate some of the tasteless dehydrated food, but could manage no more than a mouthful or two. The memory of the corpse was still too fresh.

When he had cleaned his mouth out with water, and swilled his face down, he returned to the canoe. In the heat of the day it had dried, and Wentik saw that although the tools used to carve it out had been crude, the wood was sound and the design was solid. There would be little chance of it overturning unless he encountered rapids.

He pushed it down to the water, took the paddle and worked his way out into the stream.

Almost at once he started drifting downstream and he crawled into the stern of the canoe. The actual paddling was not easy to master, and the craft swung round several times in midstream before he got the knack.

As soon as he was moving in a manner which he felt was most

under his control, he stopped paddling and took out the insect-repellent cream. Again, he smeared it over his face and arms.

In about half a mile the stream widened, and the sun fell on him. Although trees and creepers still overhung the water there was a feeling of space, and he felt confident of finding the main Aripuana river before nightfall. From there he would have little difficulty in reaching either the village or the mission. He relaxed in the stern of the canoe, and swept on down to the confluence at a steady five miles an hour.

He didn't see the corpse again. Although he must have overtaken it within minutes of climbing into the canoe, either it had sunk, had been eaten by some denizen of the river or had decomposed to such an extent that its contact with the water had caused it to disintegrate altogether.

The fauna of the river were either less abundant or less evident than those of the land. Whatever the reason, Wentik saw very few things that could actually menace him. He had read in the past of the *piranha-fish* which was found in all rivers of the Amazonia, and a school of which could strip the flesh from a man's body in seconds. He'd heard too of giant alligators and water-snakes, which, peaceable enough when left alone, could kill a man effortlessly if provoked. But he saw none of these.

The actual task of paddling – confined mainly to keeping the canoe on a straight beam, and maintaining a careful watch out for obstructions in the water – was light, and allowed him time to think for the first time since leaving Jexon.

The most comforting aspect of his present situation was, of course, that however alien this landscape may be to him, it was his own time. That if he could somehow get back to England he would see it, but for the war, as he always had.

It was hard to conceive of the war. With major upheavals, it takes more than mere reportage to convince someone subjectively involved that the event has in fact taken place. He had read of the war in the books, and Jexon had told him of it. To the Brazilians, the new Brazilians of the twenty-second century, the war was not only fact, it was history.

But to Wentik, the knowledge of a fact could not necessarily convey to him its whole import. For he was subjectively involved.

In London, his family. In the north of England, his parents. In Sussex, his college. In west London, the firms he'd worked for. But even more than this, a whole set of memories and impressions and images which go to make up an identity. For Wentik to accept the destruction of all this would be to condone the removal of a part of himself.

His world went on unchanged ...

After two hours on the river he came to the confluence, and sailed on down the slightly more turbulent waters of the Aripuana. Consulting his maps he kept to the right bank, and in another three hours came across the Roman Catholic mission.

Moored near the bank was a medium-sized aircraft on floats. Wentik looked at it with pleasure. His quest was to be shorter than he had anticipated.

Twenty-two

•

In his office at the University, Jexon had built a symbolic socio-mechanic model of the structure of the new Brazilian society. It rested on a table opposite his desk, looking like a random collection of coloured plastic tubes and globes; each one representative of some section of the society. For each trade, profession or vocation there was a globe. And for each art, each social service, the farmers, the shopkeepers, each branch of the administration, the students, the unemployed, the sick. And where sections interacted there was a tube symbolizing the contact, its width representative of the amount of interaction.

Altogether, the sculpture resembled most nearly a plastic approximation of a complex heavy-element molecule. It was the joy of Jexon's life, having occupied in one way or another most of his waking hours since he had received his doctorate.

One way and another: only in the last few years had his sociological theories resolved themselves into anything near to concrete imagery, so making practicable the building of his model.

And even now it wasn't complete. Nor, he feared, would it ever be in his lifetime. Even his students would have difficulty in carrying on his work. Only someone with a brain like his, one that could visualize society as coherently as he, could take over.

On the table where it lay, it was surrounded by several more of the globes – tiny, irrelevant sections of his society he had yet to fit somehow into context.

It was these globes, no more than a couple of dozen, that lay between him and the completion of the model.

When he returned from the Planalto jail, Jexon fretted irritably in his office, trying to concentrate his thoughts on his work, trying to recapture the placidity and order of his progress before Wentik had turned up so unexpectedly.

He sent a plane and a crew back to the jail to wait for Wentik to return, then tried again to concentrate.

To get just another globe into the scheme ... It would mean, perhaps, reshaping almost half of the work he had done already. It wasn't a question of merely tacking the remaining globes haphazardly into the structure; each one had to have its proper place, in such a way that it reacted and interreacted with all the others.

Musgrove should be here ...

But he was in hospital, had let him down badly about Wentik. At one point, Jexon telephoned the hospital to see when Musgrove would be able to get back to his work, and was told that Musgrove was still under intensive rehabilitation treatment.

For two days, Jexon worked. He saw a way of fitting into the structure the globe that represented civilian security organizations, seeing that it necessitated the removal and rebuilding of about forty per cent of those globes already in place, and the repositioning of at least twenty more in the part not directly affected.

His forehead contracted characteristically, and he bent over the model, trying to dispel an unresolved nagging somewhere at the back of his mind. It was to do with Wentik, and he knew it ...

On the third day, his concentration was completely distracted. When he came into his office in the morning he sat at his desk, looking moodily at the model, seeing but not absorbing the subdeties of its construction.

It was Wentik's headache that was at the root of it. Wentik had breathed the disturbance gas at the jail, thinking he was immune, but it had nevertheless affected him. And now he was two hundred years in the past, alone in the jungle like Musgrove before him.

But it was necessary ... One day, the symbolic model of his society would be neat and symmetrical, each part cohesive in its place. But while the disturbance gas was allowed to remain in the atmosphere, nothing could make his society perfect. It was a random factor. And it was Wentik that could derandomize it. Wentik, or this man he says knows more about it.

They must be here to put things right. Everything depended upon it.

Something didn't fit . . .

It was as if Wentik hadn't understood about the war, and how he was escaping it. But he had read the histories, hadn't he? Surely he could see that a return to his old life would be impossible now?

As Jexon sat at his desk, looking at the model in front of him, he wondered whether Wentik would ever appreciate the importance he had already played in moulding this society, or the work he could still do here. What had to be done was perhaps trivial, yet the disturbance gas undeniably existed and made a palpable contribution to life here.

But there was still a loose end or two. Particularly Wentik's assertion that his work was unfinished, that this assistant of his had done the work.

But had he? If Wentik found the man, N'Goko, brought him here to the present, *someone* would have to carry on the work after him. Or else the disturbance gas and the society it had helped to form, *this* society, would cease suddenly to exist. Suppose it wasn't N'Goko at all that had done the work, but someone else. Even a scientist working somewhere else at another time; or even for the other side?

Perhaps Wentik's quest, taking him even now to his old laboratory, was inherently fated.

And yet . . .. He seemed to be the key to it all. Certainly he knew of the gas, how it would work, the effects it would have in practice. If he could do nothing else, he would be able to find some way of counteracting its effects on Brazilian life today.

Suddenly, Jexon saw clearly that whatever else happened, Wentik would have to be brought back here, whether it was with or without this other man. Just as he had done a few years before, he realized again that it was Wentik, and only Wentik, who could help him bring his own work to completion. Nothing else mattered. If he were to realize, as Jexon himself had done, that going back to look for someone who had completed his research was not going to work, then he may well choose not to come back at all.

Two things were incontrovertible. First, that the disturbance gas existed. And secondly, that Wentik would be able to do something about it, given opportunity and incentive.

Jexon thought carefully for another hour, then lifted his communicator, and made the first of several calls. When he left his office a day later and went to the airport where his personal jet was waiting for him, he left behind on the table an uncompleted plastic model, surrounded by the globes that, so far, he had been unable to fit into place.

Twenty-three

•

Wentik spent the night in the mission hospital, alone and upset. The war was a fact, the Portuguese radio station broadcasting from Manaus spoke of nothing else. At the mission there was an air of deep sadness and mourning. In the tiny white chapel set back from the river on a wide lawn, the black-vestmented fathers said Mass at midnight; a solemn requiem to the dead of the world that had shaken Wentik's outer shell and brought true grief into his experience for the first time.

Afterwards, alone in the humid dark of the hospital ward, exhausted yet unable to sleep, he found himself tormented by images of his wife. The implications of his relationship with the nurse, Karena, suddenly became all too real, emphasized by the solemn mood of the mission. Perhaps it was this alone, or perhaps it was the effect of the disturbance gas still weakening his will to resist influence.

It was possible that as he lay here in Brazil, Jean was still alive. If this were so, then he had betrayed her.

The Catholic doctrine, sounding in the clearing by the silent-flowing river, a melancholy affirmation of trust in God and the spirit of man, had no two views on adultery. Wentik, by no means a religious man, found himself in sympathy with the belief, and when he wept in his bed that night it was not for himself or for the dead being mourned by the priests, but for Jean.

In the morning he spoke to one of the fathers about the aircraft.

The priest was distracted, vague.

'We use it to help the sick,' he said. 'Without it we would have no transport across the jungle. We can use boats on the river, but there is no other way . . .'

Wentik thought quickly. This was something Jexon had not foreseen. There were several aircraft in this part of Brazil, and the currency he had would more than pay for them. But they were a vital part of existence here.

'Are there any other aircraft I could have?'

The priest shrugged; his attention was elsewhere. 'There is the plantation at Manicore,' he said. 'But that is hundreds of miles.'

'Could you fly me there?'

'We need the aircraft. If the war comes to Brazil there will be many sick. We cannot be without it.'

How could he tell him he knew the war would not come? That the worst that would happen would be the fall-out, and that that was several weeks away?

An idea came into his mind. If Jexon could do this . . .

'Father,' he said. 'Can I *borrow* the plane? I will need it only a few days. Then I will return it to you. You can have most of my money, and we will give you a second plane as a gift a few weeks later.'

The priest stared down the river. 'Is it for the war that you want it?'

'No,' said Wentik. 'Not the war. If anything, what I can do will shorten it.'

'Shorten the war?'

Wentik nodded. During the night he had made something of a tentative plan, to use the aircraft to get him back to England somehow. Jexon's quest had seemed trivial in comparison with his new feelings. But faced with the simple, abstracted severity of the priest, he knew he had to go on.

'I can fly it to . . . to a man who is working for the Americans. If I can stop his work, the war will be less severe.'

'You are not an American?'

'No. British.'

'And this man. You say he is an American?'

'He's a Nigerian.'

The priest nodded slowly. 'I am *Belgique.* Of Belgium. The Americans are very evil?'

'No,' said Wentik. 'This war is no one's fault. It is inevitable.' As time itself is unalterable, so is the progress of events. The priest said suddenly: 'Wait here.'

He hurried away towards the mission, and disappeared into its interior. For ten minutes Wentik stood alone on the lawn that sloped down to the river, looking at the blue and white aircraft bobbing at its mooring on the river.

The father returned, and said: 'You will return our plane in one week?'

'Yes.'

'And let us have another?'

'Yes.'

'Then take it. We do not want money.'

'But I can give you thirty thousand dollars.'

The priest shook his head firmly. 'It is American money.'

'No,' said Wentik, thinking of it lying in the vaults of a ruined Washington bank for two hundred years before the Brazilians found it. 'It is from Brazil. It was – converted into dollars because we thought it would be acceptable.'

The priest looked hesitant.

'Take it,' Wentik pressed. 'It will build another hospital, perhaps.'

'Why do you wish to give this to us?'

'I'm desperate,' Wentik said. 'I need the aircraft, and you can use the money. Please take it.'

He took the satchel from his back, and dropped it on the lawn. He took out the money and laid it on the grass in a neat pile.

Another man had come out of the mission, and was standing with the father.

'This is Father Molloy,' the priest said. 'He will show you how to handle the aircraft.'

Three hours later, Wentik took the plane up by himself from the river, and headed it south.

It had taken most of the intervening time to re-acclimatize himself to flying a light aircraft. Most of his logged time in the past had been on small club craft, but he had had some experience on a twin-engined Cessna which was basically the same as this.

The actual handling of the craft was sluggish and unresponsive, partly because of the huge floats attached to its undercarriage, and partly because of the heavy load of fuel he carried on board. Father Molloy had taken him on several practice take-offs and landings until satisfied that Wentik had mastered it.

The overall distance from Brazil to the Antarctic Wentik had estimated to be in the region of five thousand miles. He had fuel enough to carry him at least as far as Rio Grande, provided he could land somewhere and refuel from the spare drums he carried aboard. At Rio Grande, the fathers had assured him, he could obtain more. From there, he would be on his own.

At the Concentration there were vast supplies of fuel for the air-strip, and Wentik was confident he would be able to find enough for the return journey.

Within minutes of taking off he saw the Planalto District.

And for the first time, he saw it as a complete circle hewn out of the forest. Jexon had done as he said he would: the way back to the future was there and it was waiting for him.

He could just make out the jail as a tiny black dot at the centre of the circle. It was a long way away.

He flew on south.

An hour before nightfall he saw a broad lake, and landed on it.

There was little vegetation here, and no signs of habitation. Nevertheless he moored the plane with the heavy drop-anchor provided some hundred yards from the shore. Then he crawled out on to the wings with the fuel drums, and began the laborious task of filling it by hand. This took nearly two hours, and it was cold and dark by the time he had finished.

Shivering, he returned to the cabin, cooked himself a meal on the portable cooker in the cabin, then lay down on one of the bunks and fell asleep.

He awoke at first light, to find a heavy rainstorm building up in the east. A vast cumulonimbus, roaring up to the stratosphere in white tumbling bulges and opening into a beautiful anvil-shaped head, was less than five miles away. Forgoing breakfast, Wentik washed quickly, and within minutes was airborne.

There were several other similar clouds in the region, and Wentik flew studiously to avoid them. Keeping low, and sometimes detouring miles to stay away from their unpredictable downdraughts – in the unfamiliar and bulky aircraft he felt almost incapable of flying in anything but a straight line-ahead – it took him almost the whole of the morning to get to the coast.

By the time he found Rio Grande, and landed as directed at the northern end of the coast where a marine fuelling depot was situated, it was two in the afternoon. At first he had difficulty in getting the fuel he required; the Brazilian Navy, he was told, had requisitioned all supplies for its own use. At first at a loss to know what he should do, Wentik finally remembered that all South Americans are potentially bribable, and although it cost nearly the whole of the remainder of his cash he got what he required.

By the time he was clear of the city, and had sufficient fuel to reach Antarctica, it was almost evening. It became of first importance to reach a sheltered mooring place for the night. The farther south he went, and he was now down below the thirtieth parallel, the earlier the sunset came. In the end he landed on Lake Mirim, spreading across the Uruguayan border.

During the night, a wind sprang up from the coast, and he slept badly, fearing that the aircraft might come to harm.

In the morning, he topped up the tanks from his supply, and set off again. He flew now out into the ocean, on a southerly course.

And the immensity of his journey suddenly daunted him.

Beneath him, only four thousand feet away was the grey south Atlantic. Now he was forced to fly without rest, for there was nowhere he could land. The ocean was below, calm for the time of year, but its three-foot swells would immediately wreck any attempt to land.

All day he flew, fighting against the cramps that snatched at his leg-muscles, and taking mouthfuls of food as he was able.

An hour and a half after nightfall, in the lee of the great rocky cliffs of the Falklands, he landed the tiny craft on the smooth water of Port Stanley harbour.

He was in British territory again.

*

Wentik spent two whole days in Port Stanley, partly to recover from the flight, and partly to prepare for the last and most difficult stage.

He had hoped to be able to get news of the war, but the inhabitants knew less about it than he did. Everywhere, Wentik saw the same hopeless expression on the faces of the people as he had seen at the mission. The Falkland Islanders would probably survive the war, he thought, but that wouldn't be their worry. They depended for their livelihood and life on trade with Argentina, and if South America were to be badly hit, then they would suffer. A selfish view, maybe, but an understandable one when isolated on an outcropping of rock some four hundred miles out into the Adantic.

In Port Stanley he had extensions made to his fuel-tanks, so that he could fly farther without refuelling.

Then, on the morning of the third day, he took off from the harbour, while a crowd of the inhabitants watched from the shore. Perhaps they wondered at his destination, or automatically assumed he was flying to Argentina, but no one ever inquired.

Refreshed after his two days on land, Wentik felt totally prepared for the flight, and even on encountering a storm less than two hours from leaving, he flew on stoically.

Within an hour and a half he was through it. But now, instead of water, there was ice beneath him. And the sky was darkening.

The last part of his journey, the thousand miles over the ice, would be the hardest. For Wentik had no choice but to try to land the craft on the frozen surface of the plateau itself, and trust that the metal floats on the undercarriage of the plane would hold up as skis long enough for him to get down safely.

In the maps Jexon had given him was a detailed one of the Hollick Kenyon Plateau, showing the precise situation of the Concentration, and all its entrances. How he had possession of it, Wentik did not know. But at least it would enable him to find it with ease. Someone who did not know what he was looking for could pass over the Concentration a dozen times, and never see it.

As he flew south, the sun got lower and lower, until it seemed to skid along the horizon. The frozen sea below was lit with an oblique wash of orange light, contrasting with the dark blue of the sky above.

Now, although he had the cabin-heaters turned up full, Wentik could feel the stark chill of the Antarctic seeping into his body.

After fourteen hours, the sun was almost out of sight below the crystal-clear horizon, and the ice was a dim white radiance below. He lifted the aircraft to clear a range of low mountains, and then he was over the Hollick Kenyon Plateau.

He searched for an hour before he located the Concentration: all that could be seen from the air was a series of low metal posts scored into the ice and protruding less than six feet into the air. Like the outer ring of stones around an ancient temple, they marked the perimeter. Gratefully, Wentik circled round them and, by taking a sight on one of them, made a rough and ready estimate of wind-direction.

There was no sun, but a kind of frozen twilight gave the ice a clear luminescence of its own. It was the end of the Antarctic winter. In days, this not-light not-dark hinterland would be replaced by the daily rising and setting of the sun. And in precious few weeks after that, the sun would stay above the horizon for the whole twenty-four hours.

Wentik selected what looked to him like the smoothest stretch of ice, and made a few dummy runs over it. He would have only one go at this . . .

At last he was ready, and circled round for the final time. On this landing, he thought, a lot depended. Mentally, almost pedantically, he went through landing procedure by rote, as he'd been taught so many years ago, above the meadows of England.

He came in on his last run, the thin metal floats skimming only feet above the ice and snow. He throttled back until he was moving at the slowest permissible speed, then gentled the stick forward.

The floats touched.

And the metal crumpled, and the undercarriage buckled. Wentik slammed the throttles open, and the engines roared, but the plane had lost its flying speed. The port wing dropped, and the tip crabbed into the snow. At once, the starboard wing came up, and the nose buried itself in the snow. Wentik threw his arms up over his face as the metal bulkhead behind him folded in. The canopy shattered around him and the instruments smashed. There was a roaring, crashing noise as the wing collapsed on top of the fuselage, and the plane cartwheeled for the last time on to its back. And slid to a halt.

A cold wind, flecked with sharp crystals of ice, blew in through the wreckage.

Twenty-four

•

How long he remained unconscious, Wentik never knew. He became abruptly aware of an intense cold, and then he was fully awake.

He was lying in almost total darkness, his legs higher than the rest of his body and the bulk of his weight being borne by his shoulder-blades. His head throbbed with pain and he could feel liquid, presumably blood, on his face. Carefully, he flexed the muscles of his body to find if any bones had been broken. The only real pain he felt was from his left arm, which was caught between two pieces of the wreckage. His right arm was free.

The immediate concern must be to get under cover. Already the cold had surrounded him.

There seemed to be no way of moving from the wrecked cockpit, his body held securely in this awkward position. He pushed with his legs, but his shoulders pressed more firmly against the metal. No freedom of movement in that direction. He tried to move his legs, and found that they could kick in the confined space. His right hand was resting on a long rod of metal, presumably a part of the controls, and it seemed to be free. He clasped it.

The frame of the aircraft was constructed of wood, and this was his only hope. He lifted the metal rod, and swung it upwards. There was a splintering noise. He swung it again, and more wood broke.

In seconds he had made a sizeable hole, and he pressed his feet against the panelling. There was a noise of cracking wood and tearing canvas, and suddenly dim light spilled in. He kicked again, but stopped as the wreckage of the fuselage above and behind him began to creak.

He shuffled forward, pulling his body with the movement of his legs. When he got his waist to the hole he was forced to stop. His left arm was still trapped, and was hurting. He tugged it, and felt the flesh pull against jagged metal.

If he could only free the arm, he could get out. He tugged at it again, and felt the flesh tear. Pain shot through his arm, and he shut his eyes for a second.

Finally, in desperation, he snatched it away, shouting with pain.

He wriggled through the hole, and fell on to the surface of the ice outside. There was a strong wind blowing, and it was bitterly cold.

He looked at his arm, and saw a deep flesh wound. Blood was pouring from it. He laid it across his chest and held on to his right shoulder.

On the horizon, a black mass of cloud loomed up, blotting out all visibility. Wentik looked at it, and realized that within minutes what little light there was would be blanketed out by the blizzard. He must get under cover …

When he tried to land the aircraft, he had been aiming to stop it as near as possible to one of the entrances to the Concentration, marked by the electrically heated pole. Under the surface ice was an entrance to one of the lift-shafts that went down to the complex of tunnels.

The nearest pole was about two hundred yards away, and Wentik hurried towards it as fast as he could manage in the frozen snow. He realized now that unless he got under cover, he would have only a matter of minutes to live. Already the blood on his face had frozen, and that on his arm was threatening to. It was impossibly cold, each breath he took exploding inside his lungs.

He was running now, taking great staggering steps in the snow. He fell several times, cursing the cold and the pain and the clumsiness of his movement.

Five yards from the pole, he slipped backwards, his feet sliding out from under him and falling down. He threw out his right arm to try and balance, but slithered gracelessly into a deep trench that had been partially concealed by a drift of snow.

The entrance.

He climbed to his feet again and looked to the side. Immediately to his left the trench was covered over, becoming a tunnel under the ice-cap. He walked down it, shaking with cold. Now he was out of the wind, he could appreciate the total fury of it. He glanced back and saw that the blizzard was beginning.

After he had gone about ten yards, he came to some rough steps, and went down them. At the bottom, covered over by a sheet of corrugated steel, was a concrete platform. In front of him was a metal door, with an identity-plate. He pressed the palm of his right hand against it, and in seconds the door slid back.

Behind, was the compartment of the elevator.

He went inside, and jabbed the control to take him down.

The descent took three minutes. In that time Wentik had inspected the wound in his arm and found that, as far as he could tell, the cut was superficial. There seemed to be no arteries severed, for already the flow of blood was slower than it had been when he first looked at it.

At the bottom of the shaft the doors opened, and he found himself in one of the metal corridors that once had been so familiar to him.

He looked round for the plan of the Concentration that was at every intersection of the tunnels. He must get something done about his arm . . .

A first-aid post was marked as being some fifty yards along the side corridor, and he moved down it quickly. He threw the door open, and went inside.

The room was bare and utilitarian. Along one wall was a bed with a pile of blankets and pillows on the top, in the centre of the room was a metal table with two chairs pushed underneath its edge, and on one wall was a large cabinet containing medical equipment.

He took an elastic tourniquet and wrapped it around the upper part of his arm, tightening it until the blood stopped flowing from the wound. Then he took a tube of tissue-restorative cream from the cabinet and smeared it on, wincing at the stab of pain it induced. Finally, he found a long white bandage, and rolled it lightly round the wound until it was completely protected.

When all this was done, he took off the tourniquet, and found a linen arm-sling in the cabinet, which he put on.

Before going back into the corridor he took a heavy coat from a cupboard in the room and put it on. Although it was warmer down here than it was at the surface, it was nevertheless only just above freezing temperature in the tunnels.

He went back outside, and returned to the main corridor. Looking up and down it, he realized the one thing of importance.

The Concentration appeared to be deserted.

He consulted the map again, and set off towards his own old laboratory.

His first impression as he walked into the main research lab was the overwhelming stench. He went over to the line of cages, and looked in at the thirty or so dead rats.

He looked round the lab but could see no trace of any notes, and passed through into his old office. As he had anticipated, everywhere was deserted.

He went to his desk, and pulled open the drawers. Empty.

The filing-cabinet. Empty.

All the textbooks from the shelves had been taken. The supply of stationery had gone. The two chairs were placed tidily against the sides of the desks. The cupboard that had once contained the day-to-day notes and analyses of the research staff... empty.

In the metal waste-paper bin there was a pile of black, flaky cinders. Wentik ran his fingers through the mess, but there was no paper left from which anything could be deciphered.

Almost as soon as he had stepped out of the lift, he had felt that the entire Concentration had been evacuated. He should have known it would be, and perhaps instinctively had.

He walked out into the corridor, and headed for the nearest exit.

There is no changing of history. Was it not predestined that he should never find N'Goko here? Because what if he had? Suppose the plane had not crashed, and N'Goko was here. What then? Would he have gone with Wentik to Brazil? Would he have destroyed his notes and the products of the research he'd done in Wentik's absence?

Suppose the plan had gone as it should. Wentik and N'Goko return to Brazil and transfer to the future. There, in the São Paulo of the twenty-second century they work to destroy a gas that had been created jointly by them. And if N'Goko had gone with Wentik, would the gas have ever been used in the war? Would they have got there to find there was no longer any problem from it?

For there could surely be no tampering with reality.

The São Paulo he had visited was every bit as real as his own world of the twentieth century. Karena was real, and Jexon, and a man called Musgrove who had sampled, like Wentik, both realities. If the disturbance gas was not used in the war, would not the intrinsic nature of that new society be changed?

As time itself is unalterable, so is the progress of events.

Just as Wentik had known when he took the plane from the fathers that no action he could take would have done anything to avert the war, so he realized now that there had never been anything he could have done to prevent the use of the gas in the war. Nor, for that matter, could he have ever found N'Goko and taken him to Brazil.

He came to the nearest elevator, and stepped into it. The doors closed, and he jabbed at the button. The lift began to rise.

The Concentration was abandoned. Empty, and futile now, as Wentik's own quest.

For he was faced with failure. Perhaps not of his own causing, but at least of his own doing.

He had failed as a scientist, since his work was incomplete and had been used demonstrably to adverse purpose. He had caused the death of one man, and the probable insanity of several others. He had taken on a task for Jexon, and had not fulfilled it. He had broken the trust of the priests; they would not even get their own plane back. And, perhaps of most personal significance, he had betrayed his wife.

Utterly alone, as no man before him had been, Wentik stepped out of the elevator on the top stage, and stood in the cold.

From here, there could be nothing. A war tore at the gut of the world he had grown up in; and a second world waited for him to return.

He unbuttoned the heavy coat, and let it fall to the floor. He stood in the clothes Jexon had given him in Brazil. Lightweight city clothes totally unsuited to Antarctic weather, they gave little protection. In this dark chamber, a few feet below the level of the ice, he felt the cold at once.

Outside . . .

He looked round, aware not of the steel walls and ceiling or of the concrete floor, but a desolation of everything unseen.

He walked to the entrance, along the passage hewn out of the ice of the plateau itself, and up the steps into the night and the gale and the blizzard.

But the sun was shining from a clear sky, and the air was still, and the ice was a white so brilliant he could not see.

Dazedly, he walked away from the entrance to the Concentration, out across the frozen snow. His eyes he covered with his right forearm.

A voice said: 'Over here, Doctor Wentik.'

And he turned, and there was Jexon standing at the hatch of a silver VTOL aircraft.

Twenty-five

•

An hour and a half later, Wentik sat at the observation-port of the lounge cabin, and through the heavily tinted lenses of smoked glasses watched the white wasteland slip by below.

He had eaten a meal prepared by the steward of the aircraft, and now relaxed on a couch with a glass of wine. Jexon sat opposite him. As Wentik had eaten he had explained to him how, by a different process of thought, he reached the same process as Wentik: that events cannot be changed.

'... so I brought the plane down here as quickly as I could,' he concluded.

Wentik shook his head slowly. The transition from the readiness for personal death to an acceptance of continuing life is not an immediate one.

'In case you're wondering,' Jexon went on, 'this is 2189. The plane carries a portable displacement-field generator of its own.'

Wentik looked around the cabin. 'This is your plane?' he asked.

'Yes. I had it fitted out to my own requirements.'

It was a bigger than any of the craft he had been aboard so far. There was a crew of four: two pilots, a navigator and a cook-cum-steward who treated Jexon with a deference that was only a fraction short of servility. Suddenly, Wentik realized how high up in the government of Brazil the man must be.

'What's the range of the aircraft?' he said.

'Virtually unlimited.'

'So you came down here in one hop?'

The man nodded. 'And we'll go back that way.'

Wentik sipped his wine thoughtfully. He was still mentally in his own time; the condition of a world witnessing its own suicide, as reflected in the faces of the priests and the Falkland Islanders, seemed so much more real than the society of Jexon. After all, the disturbance gas was only a minor inconvenience soon curable. His presence in Brazil was a luxury for them; to him it was something altogether different. They could get by without him. Jexon had admitted that no one in Brazil had attempted seriously to find an antidote for the gas. Yet with their resources ... They thought they were doing him a favour; an opportunity for life instead of sure death in his own world.

But for Wentik, with the preparation for his own death still fresh in his mind, there was no question as to what he should do.

He said to Jexon: 'Take me to England.'

'Impossible!'

'I don't see why. The aircraft has the range.'

'Yes, but the whole of Europe is heavily radioactive. We couldn't land there. It would not be safe. And what would it achieve?'

Wentik looked straight at the man.

'I'm not working for you, Jexon. It means too much to me, and too little to you. I don't care about death. I just want to get home. You say this aircraft has a field-generator. Then drop me off in England.'

'But you have so much to live for in Brazil. A new life, every facility for you to carry on your work. You have even found yourself a girl—'

'Don't you talk to me about her!' Wentik flared, suddenly vocalizing what he had been thinking for days.

'But a man like you needs a wife.'

'I already have one,' Wentik said. 'And because of your social problems we've been separated.'

'You're not married.'

'I'm not?'

'Not according to the information we have on you. You lived alone in an apartment in Minneapolis, there was no mention of a wife anywhere on the government files, you were alone at the Concentration ...'

'I'm British, for God's sake,' Wentik said, too loudly. 'It was a temporary arrangement. I was due to go home five months after Musgrove arrived.'

'I didn't know this.'

'It would have made a difference if you had?' Wentik said with heavy sarcasm. 'The only thing that matters to you is your bloody society.'

Jexon said: 'That's not true! If I'd known you were married, I would never have sent Musgrove to get you.'

Wentik stared angrily out of the port. Already the plane was over the sea, a black sea liberally dotted with floating ice. Here in this world it was late Antarctic summer, and the floes were broken and free.

Jexon too had lapsed into silence, and was scribbling something on a small pad of white paper on a table at the side of the couch. He appeared to be counting something.

There was this long silence between the two, and while it continued Wentik watched the sea until there was no more ice. He took off the dark glasses, and glanced at his arm. It was still in a sling, but was no longer giving him as much pain as it had. The graze on his scalp had stopped bleeding almost as soon as it had started, but a sizable area of his hair was matted with blood. He looked forward to using the luxurious bathroom he had seen at the rear end of the plane. He said: 'What are you writing?'

'I'm calculating something,' Jexon replied. 'I'm almost finished. Have you any idea what the date is?'

'Somewhere around the middle of August, I think.'

'The fourteenth, probably. Or the fifteenth. It's not positive, because of the distortion. We never know how many days exactly will be traversed in the displacement-field. Did you find out what the date was while you were there?'

'It never occurred to me.'

'A pity. It would have helped, because the distortion accumulates. As it is, I'll have to estimate a lot.'

'What are you doing?'

'I'm trying to help you. We'll assume that the date today is the fifteenth. It will take us two days to get to England from here if we fly direct. That makes it the seventeenth. Say the eighteenth, to be on the safe side.'

'The safe side of what?'

'The bombing. I'm trying to re-unite you with your family.'

'That's impossible. The war had already started.'

Jexon nodded slowly.' In America it has. But there was a lull in the bombing. The first nuclear weapons in Europe were not detonated until the twenty-second of August.'

Western Europe laid waste in the second wave of bombing . . .

'Your family's still alive, Doctor Wentik.'

But he wasn't listening. He was looking out of the port, watching the sea slip by below, and planning what he should do.

Late the following day, the aircraft was flying above the North Atlantic, parallel with the coast of north-western Africa. They had passed over little land, and Wentik was already bored with the endless sea. At times he moved restlessly about the cabin, while Jexon watched with some concern. Once the two men had agreed on details of what they would do when they arrived in England, they had little to discuss, and Wentik was thrown back to his own thoughts. The possibility of seeing his family again now swollen to near-certainty, the feeling of insecurity that had become a part of his existence faded for the first time since meeting Musgrove and Astourde.

He spent part of the day in reading again Jexon's book concerning the structure of the new Brazilian society. It intrigued him in the way any novelty is likely to, though the breathtaking liberalism of its practices had the elements of fanaticism in some of the details, like the eighteenth-century religious and moral Utopias.

He read it, though, with a sense of duty, since he felt he should prepare for his new life.

His decision had been made: that he and his family would return with Jexon to São Paulo and try to find some way of counteracting the effects of the disturbance gas.

Some of the claims of the book intrigued him. There appeared to be no formal government; decisions on all levels were left to the people directly involved. Where doubt or disagreement occurred, the next higher social stratum was consulted. The larger the problem, the higher it had to go and the more people there were involved. The actual stratification of the society was ill-defined by the book, and he was tempted to question Jexon about it. The only time he did so, however, the man's passionate interest in the subject revealed itself, and the substance of the answer was lost on Wentik.

The strata seemed to be defined by personal merit or achievement, though how the differentiations were actually made was not indicated.

Wentik considered the apparent wealth of Jexon: the private aircraft and crew, the position of authority he held at the hospital and university. If the book were to be understood, the man was a meritocrat-advocate, interpreter and delineator of a society he had abstracted himself.

When he had finished the book, and he and Jexon had eaten a meal, he asked the man how different life would be for him and his family in São Paulo.

Jexon's countenance brightened, like that of a scholar whose subject is raised in debate.

'Superficially, none at all. Day-to-day existence is much the same as I imagine it would have been in your own time. It is only authority that is decentralized.'

'But there must be some difference.'

Jexon nodded. 'There is. In an executive sense. Take for example the decision to bring you to Brazil. It was entirely my own. I discussed the whole project with Musgrove before we started, but it was my authority that set things going. I had access to what I thought was the complete information on you, and acted within the scope of my experience.'

'And things went wrong,' Wentik said. 'Doesn't that imply to you, as a sociologist, that there is a flaw in the system?'

'Perhaps,' Jexon agreed. 'But then this was a rather special set of circumstances. The only real flaw that exists, and one, incidentally, which doesn't bother many people, is that it sometimes happens that the right hand doesn't know what the left is doing. Typical of this was when you arrived in São Paulo. Not only were you taken to the hospital in error, but poor Musgrove was held by the police until we discovered the mistake.'

Jexon paused, and considered.

'Life in Brazil,' he went on, ' is a lot less oppressive, I think, than the kind of existence to which you were accustomed. The inhibitions you would take for granted, like sexual or interpersonal ones, just do not exist.'

'It sounds too good to be true,' Wentik said quietly, thinking of Karena.

'Perhaps it does, to your ears. But it works, as you will see when we get back.'

Wentik looked through the port, and saw in the growing darkness the lights of a town on the coast some ten miles away to the East. A part of Africa, unknown and impossibly remote. Would he stay in Brazil? he wondered. To Jexon, caught up in the esoteric scientist's world of theories and abstract concepts, perhaps the society was a source of constant delight. But to Wentik it could never be more than an escape. A haven made open to him by circumstance; a way to avoid a certain death from nuclear blast or radioactive fall-out. He looked back at Jexon and saw a proud old man with eyes full of burning intelligence ... or was it another, more fanatical, kind of gleam? These people and their fathers had survived the holocaust, and human civilization was recovering. Was he, Elias Wentik, to take a part in that?

Twenty-six

•

England from the air, to Wentik's critical eye, had changed tragically in two hundred years.

Soon after waking, he and Jexon watched the coast slip by below. The weather was drab and grey, with a cloud-base of about two thousand feet. At Wentik's request, the pilot flew the aircraft slowly along the coastline at a height of five hundred feet. Everywhere, untidy growths of trees and unkempt bushes helped conceal the ruins of the buildings. They passed over what had once been a large town – Wentik thought it was Bournemouth, but he wasn't sure – and saw no movement anywhere.

After ten minutes they flew inland, Wentik depressed against his expectation at the sight of the familiar countryside. Yet was it so familiar? The England he knew was populated, cared for, congested. This place ...

The navigator appeared at the door to the lounge cabin.

'The background gamma-radiation count is high, sir,' he said to Jexon. 'But not lethal.'

'Thank you.'

Jexon was looking at a map of this part of England. An old one, Wentik noticed, one that had towns and roads marked upon it.

Jexon said, passing the map across: 'I think here, where I've marked. It's the eastern edge of the Salisbury Plain, near Amesbury.'

Wentik said: 'Does it have to be so far from London?'

'I'm afraid so. You've got to remember that the England of your time is in the middle of a war. If our craft suddenly appeared in the middle of a well-populated area, there's no telling what might happen. I think this is the nearest we can get to London with safety.'

Wentik thought for a moment, then finally agreed.

Jexon depressed a half-concealed button, and in seconds the navigator had returned.

'Would you bring us down here,' he said. He gave the map to the man, who nodded and went back into the control section of the craft. A few moments later, the aircraft changed direction.

Jexon said: 'The displacement-field generator that I have on this craft is rather more sophisticated than the one at the jail. That one was large because it doubled as a Direct Power generator. The one I have here has the advantage of being fairly portable, and the area of the actual field displaced is adjustable to a certain degree. The only snag with it is that the distortion-factor is larger.'

'Will that make a difference?'

'I shouldn't think so. We've got plenty of latitude.'

Wentik shrugged. It seemed to matter little now.

After about ten minutes, the note of the aircraft's engines changed again, and the ground appeared to float up slowly towards them. Jexon got to his feet.

'Come on,' he said.

He walked down towards the tail of the aircraft, past the tiny but luxuriously appointed staterooms and into a rather more utilitarian cabin. Here, amid a long instrument-console, was the field-generator.

Wentik climbed down from the main hatch, and stood on the grass. It was long, and the cold February wind from the southwest rustled it around his feet. Before him, this tiny section of Salisbury Plain stretched away. Two hundred yards in front of him, it rose up to a small hill, overgrown with bushes and trees. On each side of the hill, the plain went on untidily towards the horizon. Jexon had set the field for a diameter of less than half a mile, but from where Wentik was standing he could not see any really noticeable sign of the terminator.

Jexon was standing behind him, in the hatch.

'How long will you need?' he said.

Wentik considered. 'Until tomorrow evening. It may be longer, but I'm not sure.'

Jexon gave him the map. He said: 'If you walk that way,' pointing towards the hill, 'you'll come to one of your main roads in about a mile. We're here on the map. That road will take you into London.'

Wentik nodded.

'Now is there anything else?'

'I don't think so.'

Jexon put out his hand, and the two men shook awkwardly.

'Be as quick as you can,' Jexon said. 'We're exposed here. I don't want to attract unwelcome attention.' He looked round at the green vegetation, so different from that of Brazil.

'Good luck, Doctor Wentik.'

Wentik nodded again. There was nothing to say. He turned away, and set off towards the main road.

He decided to go over the top of the hill itself. It wasn't steep, and the effort of the climb would be more than repaid by the wide view he would gain from its summit. He walked quickly, the unconscious frustration of the last two days manifesting itself into haste. He had something to do, and the sooner it was completed the better.

He started up the hill, and in very few minutes reached the top.

The trees were in leaf . . .

The far slope of the hill was covered in bushes and trees, and in contrast with the part of the plain he had just been on, was covered in an abundance of greenery.

And it was warmer. Mid-August.

He looked back, and saw Jexon standing at the side of the aircraft. That man, thought Wentik, is two hundred years away. An anachronism in the English countryside. He looked down at the clothes he wore; the featureless grey of the close-fitting material. Or is it I who am out of place?

The view from the top of the hill extended for miles in all directions. Jexon's craft lay to the south, and beyond it the sky was bright with the light from the sun. The plain was unlike the other one he had grown so accustomed to in Brazil: this was wooded and green, and it undulated irregularly, in a multitude of different shades.

He turned, and looked towards where Jexon had told him the road would be. Here the ground was more level, dropping down from the hill in a fairly smooth slope. There was a copse of trees about half a mile from the hill, then a fence. Beyond that, two or three cultivated fields, and a straight line of trees, evidently growing along the side of the road.

Wentik started walking down towards it.

It was a light, quiet English afternoon. The war and Jexon and Brazil suddenly felt incredibly remote. He had forgotten how easy it was to walk.

It took him less than ten minutes to reach the road. He climbed over a low wooden fence, and scrambled down a grassy bank to the side of the road. On each side of him, the road stretched away, lined on both sides by tall trees.

There was no traffic.

In the unexpected still, Wentik stood for a moment, uncertain now of what he should do. His plan had been to stop a passing vehicle and get a lift into London. He puzzled about it for a few more seconds, then started walking.

Almost at once, he heard the noise of an engine, and stopped. Coming up from behind him, from the west and going towards London, was a car. He waited until it came into sight, then walked out into the middle of the road and waved both his arms.

It was a large white station-wagon, travelling along the road at seventy miles an hour, or more. When the driver saw Wentik he braked at once, and the car stopped next to him.

Inside were two policemen.

They both leaped out, and went over to him. To his sudden unaccountable alarm Wentik saw that they were wearing heavy metal helmets on their heads, and were armed.

'What are you doing here?' one of them said.

Wentik said: 'I'm trying to get to London.'

'What the devil for?'

He looked round desperately. Something had gone wrong. He said: 'I've been away. I want to get home.'

'Let's see your papers.'

'What papers?'

The policemen held out his hand. 'Your identity and travel-permit.'

'I told you. I've been away. I haven't got any papers.'

'Where have you been to?'

Wentik thought quickly. 'America,' he said.

The two policemen looked at each other.

'America's been bombed,' one of them said.

Wentik looked round again. There was a dreadful abnormality about this interrogation on the side of a quiet road in deserted countryside.

He said: 'Look, I can explain everything. But I must get to London straight away. Can you take me there?'

The policeman shook his head slowly.

'London's been evacuated. All entry to it is sealed off.'

'*Evacuated*?' he said incredulously. 'Then where—?'

'There are a few people left. Mostly those connected with the government. And they're in shelters.'

Wentik said: 'What's the date today?'

The policeman replied: '22nd August.'

There is a distortion in the displacement-field . . .

Wentik said: 'But the bombing . . .'

'We know.'

There was a sudden ringing noise from inside the police car, and one of the men went over to it. He reached inside and pulled out a two-way speaker. He listened at it for a moment, then put it back inside.

The other man looked at him.

Wentik said: 'Can you tell me where my family are?'

'Where in London did they live?'

'Hampstead.'

The policeman pulled a booklet from his breast pocket, and leafed through it.

'They're probably in Hertfordshire. I can't say where. Every major city in Britain has been evacuated in the last week.'

The other man had returned, and he came over to Wentik and took his arm in a tight grip.

He said to the first policeman: 'That was the last alert. We've got about twenty minutes.'

Desperately, Wentik swung his arm and scrambled backwards towards the grassy bank. The policeman dived at him, but Wentik moved sharply to the side. He ran up the bank, and threw himself bodily over the fence. In the long grass on the other side he rolled over and stood up, and began running away. The two policemen clambered up the bank after him, but made no attempt to climb over the fence.

Wentik ran until he reached the far side of the field, then stopped and looked back. The two men were watching him. As soon as they saw he had stopped they disappeared from view down the bank. A few seconds later he heard the engine of the car start up.

It accelerated away, and in less than half a minute the sound of its engine could no longer be heard. The day was silent around him.

He started back towards the hill, walking slowly. London had been evacuated, as had all the other cities. Jean was somewhere in Hertfordshire, waiting, with the rest of the population, for a war which must inevitably come. In the meantime, the summer went on unknowingly.

At the top of the hill he stopped, and looked northwards across the countryside. Then he turned, and looked down at the silver aircraft waiting for him to return.

He stood there for half an hour, while the cold February winds blew up from the plain, and the warm August sun came down on his face and shoulders. And then there was a brilliant flash of light low down on the southern horizon, and two more in quick succession to its right and left.

A minute later a deep-throated rumble of sound, like distant thunder on an autumn evening, came through the air and for a moment the countryside seemed to freeze. It grew quiet as he watched the clouds spread in the distance, black and tall.

Wentik shut his eyes, and listened for more thunder.

As evening came on, he settled himself against the trunk of a tree and watched the silver aircraft below. Only as the sun was setting did a man in a lime-green cape come to the hatch and look round at the sky, now a deep blue streaked with black. He stood looking at it, then went back inside.

And half a minute later, the aircraft disappeared.